ANGELS LOVE DONUTS

A BOOK ABOUT DYING
THAT WILL CHANGE THE WAY YOU LIVE

A Novella

Leon McWhorter & Alan C. Elliott

Angels Love Donuts

CrossWise Productions Edition, 2013
PO Box 1169, Cedar Hill TX 75106
alanelliott.com/novels

Chapter 1

After parking his car in front of the Lone Star Donut Shop on a hot September morning in Dallas, a rather rotund customer ordered a double-shot espresso and two jelly-filled glazed donuts. Balancing his purchase in both hands and carrying a copy of *the Dallas Morning News* under one arm, he salivated his way to a small booth in the back of the shop. He gently placed the Styrofoam plate holding the warm, jelly-filled, sugar-saturated pastries and his hot cup of coffee on the table then slid his newspaper down beside the plate. A sudden chill rippled through his 350-pound frame as he settled into the red Naugahyde seat. He took a deep breath and noticed his donuts going in and out of focus.

It would be incorrect to blame the jelly-filled donuts or the double-shot espresso for his unfortunate death. His demise resulted from forty-something years of temporal pleasures gone awry. In his lifetime he had enjoyed 25,551 packages of filtered cigarettes, 2.2 tons of french fries, 13,000 slices of American and cheddar cheese, 7,000 bags of barbeque potato chips, and uncountable cans of light beer. On this particular September morning, as he gasped his last breath, the donut shop customer saw someone or something standing next to him. Then he slumped over in sudden and massive cardiac arrest.

Fifteen minutes passed before an impatient woman wanting to sit at the booth noticed the customer's lack of movement and reported the incident to the management. The EMS crew arrived within five minutes, tested for vital signs and made a vain attempt to revive the corpse with several jolts from a defibrillator. They didn't notice that although he had never tasted his morning donuts, a large juicy bite had been taken out of one of them.

Early the next morning at the very same donut shop, a short man wearing a black-and-yellow Hawaiian shirt and the smile of a kid in a candy store entered the Lone Star Donut Shop. He gawked at the case filled with sugary confections, ordered a box of a dozen jelly-filled donuts, placed a twenty-dollar bill on the counter, and vanished before the cashier could give him change.

That same morning, across town in a Dallas megamansion, John Alfred Money stared at his nose in the mirror.

A wayward hair poking out of his nostril was doing its best to avoid the grasp of the tweezers in John's hand. Contorting his face to get a good position, John manipulated the tweezer tines to close in on the offending hair.

Vanessa stood at the door of the bathroom, watching the drama. After twenty-three years of marriage, she was used to such acts of vanity. "Give it up, John -- come down to breakfast."

"Just a moment... I've got it. I got it."

Moments later John triumphantly held the loosened nose hair before him like a tiny trophy. He walked out of the bathroom to show off his prize, but the bedroom was empty.

At the first landing on her way down the stairs, Vanessa scooped up her West Highland white terrier, and at the bottom of the stairs, she saw Martha setting the table for breakfast.

"Good morning, Mrs. Money."

The Westie knew the morning routine. She squirmed out of Vanessa's arms and ran to Martha.

"Sit, Mitzy."

Mitzy's obedience earned her a dog snack that looked and smelled a lot like bacon, although the manufacturer had somehow managed to make the morsel also clean the canine's teeth.

Vanessa smiled. "If only everyone in this household were as easy to please. Set an extra plate for Kelly. She said she might come by this morning."

As Martha went to the kitchen to get another plate, somewhere very far away, in the ethereal bliss of heaven, a short, stocky angel wearing a black-and-yellow Hawaiian shirt strolled down a marble corridor munching on a jelly-filled donut. Under his arm he held a white donut box stamped with a "Lone Star Donuts" emblem. He paused for a moment at a door framed in gold trim and labeled with a silver sign at the side that read Receiving. He peeked in.

"You wanted to see me, big guy?"

Bartholomew looked up from his silver crystal desk. "Yes, A.D., please come in."

With a quick gulp, the stocky angel finished off his donut. He licked strawberry jelly off his fingertips and stepped into the cavernous office, extending his hand to the head angel. Bartholomew passed him a handkerchief.

The stocky angel wiped his hands as he sat in the chair facing the desk. He placed the box of donuts on the desk, sat down and put his feet up next to the box, He removed the confections quickly following a stern look from the head angel.

"So, what's up, boss man?"

"Yes, well...I'd like to review today's list before you head out."

The stocky angel raised his hand. "Hang on, cheese. I know in the past I've picked up a few out of sequence, but..."

"You realize, A.D., there is a specific reason for the pickup order."

A.D. chuckled. "Admit it—I've saved some processing time for Shipping by fudging the timeline."

Bartholomew was not without understanding. He considered the statement for a moment. "While that may be true, to our clients, time can be very important. In any case, it's always prudent to follow procedure as..."

"...as close as I can," finished A.D. "No problemo. Now, how we looking today?"

Bartholomew handed a clipboard to the angel. "A standard list...we like to give you the (he coughed) easy cases."

The stocky angel opened his box of donuts and selected a grape-jelly-filled glazed pastry as he studied the list. When he closed the box and bit down on the donut at the same time, a glob of jelly squirted out, landing smack dab in the middle of the client list. A.D. wiped the goo with the handkerchief. "Oops, sorry about that."

Bartholomew shook his head.

Through purple smudges, the angel read his list. "Let me take a look-see. Uh, Adams, Ellis...Garza, Lar? No, Low. Oh, I see it now. It's Lawson. Gladys M. Lawson. Uh-oh, this next one's a tad messy. Is it Maaa? No wait, Moo? The angel rubbed the page with his finger. Yeah. It's Money! Now there's a name, huh, Money! As in the love of..."

He looked up to see that Bartholomew was not amused. He was standing up...an indication it was time for A. D. to be gone.

"Oh...well...I guess I should..."

"You should...be about the pickups."

"Bingo..."

Bartholomew placed a hand on the angel's shoulder. "This time make a concerted effort to stay on task."

The stocky angel looked shocked. "A tasking I will go." He extended the box toward Bartholomew. "Donut?"

"No, thanks, I'm on my way to join the welcoming banquet. And you..."

"...I'm off to work."

"I'll be watching..."

"...I'll be tasking."

The stocky angel turned and took a single step. An elevator door opened out of nothingness. He stepped in and struggled to open the donut box with one hand while holding the clipboard in the other.

The elevator operator waited with some impatience. "Destination?"

"Yes…Earth, please…" He glanced at the first name on the clipboard. "Let's start with Phoenix. I hear it's beautiful this time of year. Not too hot."

The elevator operator reached for a button on the panel next to the door but stopped when the angel interrupted.

"On the other hand, wait a sec. Make it Dallas. I think I'll pay a visit to this guy named Money. Besides, there's a little donut shop on Beckley Avenue in Dallas I'd like to visit again."

"This time make a concerted effort to stay on task."

Chapter 2

Austin Townsend held a piece of buttered multigrain wheat toast in his hand and stared across the table at his girlfriend, who was holding an opened cranberry cream lipstick case halfway between the cafeteria table and her lips. Her eyes were beautiful and blue, he thought, and they were staring somewhere into space.

Austin ventured to break the spell. "Hello—earth to Kelly—are you with me? Want a nibble...of my toast?"

Kelly turned her blue eyes toward Austin and twisted the lipstick case until the cranberry cream disappeared into a silver tube. "I told you, I'm having breakfast at home this morning. I've got to prepare myself. You've got to help me think of what to say."

"That again?"

"Yes, that."

"Oh....that!" Austin waved his toast in the air with a grand gesture.

Kelly frowned. "Don't make fun of me. You know it's important." She snatched the toast from his hand and dropped it onto his plate.

He licked the crumbs from his fingers. "Okay, okay. Let's look at it this way. Do you feel confident about your call?"

"Never more confident about anything in my life...."

"So what's the problem?"

Kelly sat up straight. "Okay, here's how you can help me. Pretend to be my father."

"Your father?"

"Yes."

Austin coughed and said in a low Darth Vader voice, "I am your father, Kelly."

"No, that's not his voice. Try to look stern...and bald." She laughed.

Austin pointed two fingers at Kelly's eyes and then at his own. "Kelly...you must focus."

"Okay. I'm focusing." She forced the smile from her face. "Dad?"

"Yes, dear."

"I've been thinking."

"No!" Austin beat a fist on the table and sent his sausage patty flying off his plate and onto the floor. "Oops!" Several students sitting around them watched him peel the errant object off the sticky floor and put it back onto his plate.

"What do you mean, no?"

"Kelly, you can't start out by saying you've been thinking. That diminishes the impact. This isn't something you think about, this is something you know."

"You're right. I do know. I'm confident. I know exactly what I'm doing..."

"There you go. Unwavering. Gutsy. That's the Kelly I know. Try it again."

"Okay...Dad?"

"Yes, dear."

"I, uh...well, you better sit down, Dad."

Austin took a deep breath. "Kelly, your dad will understand if you present it right."

"My dad? Understand?"

"Absolutely...have faith."

"Faith, I have. It's my completely close-minded hardheaded father I doubt."

"What's to doubt? This is a higher calling."

"Right. Well, you've never gone toe-to-toe with the master negotiator John A. Money. The only call he cares about is the one from his stockbroker."

"Middle name A., huh? Does that stand for Austin?"

"No...it stands for Always-knows-he's-right!"

***

Four and a half miles away, in the dining room of the Money megamansion, maid Martha placed a plate and silverware on the table for Kelly. She glanced over to Vanessa, who sat at the table sipping her coffee.

"You're sure you want me to go the healthy route today?" Martha asked.

"Absolutely. Keep it low fat, high fiber."

"You expect him to sit still for this?"

"It's for his own good."

The intercom crackled, and an unhappy male voice growled from the speaker, "Vanessa! Where's my blue tie?"

Vanessa walked to the intercom and looked for help from Martha, who whispered, "In the closet."

Vanessa pushed the intercom switch. "It's in the closet, dear."

The intercom answered back, "I'm in the closet, dear!"

Martha whispered, "In the plastic dry cleaners bag by his suits, where I always leave them."

Vanessa answered into the box, "Look beside the..."

Before she could finish, the voice bellowed from upstairs, "Never mind...I found it!"

Vanessa flipped up the intercom switch. "Another morning in paradise."

As Martha set a folded napkin beside Kelly's plate, heavy footsteps descended the stairs. They were attached to a thin bald man in an expensive suit. John A. Money stood at the bottom of the staircase, tie in one hand and holding up a flimsy plastic cleaning bag in the other.

"Martha... Do you see this dry cleaning bag? Now I ask you, what kind of a place is a dry cleaning bag to put ties? Ties go on a tie rack!"

Martha opened her mouth to answer, but John continued, "That is why it is called a tie rack. Is this really that tough, Martha?"

"Yes, sir. I mean..."

"Let me be specific. Pick up the cleaning, take the ties to the closet, take them out of the plastic bag, and place them on the tie rack. Then when I need a tie, I go to the closet, and voilà...I find a tie."

"Yes, sir."

"Now, did I go too fast? Let's hit the highlights...cleaning bag, tie..."

Vanessa intervened. "Let it go, John. You have your silly tie."

John saw in Vanessa's face the look that meant "drop this or sleep alone in the guest room for the next month." "I was just trying to say... Okay. Okay...Martha, I'm sorry. I have a lot on my mind this morning, and I don't have time for tie hunts."

"May I get you some breakfast?" asked Martha in her most professional voice.

"Please."

Martha walked back into the kitchen, and John planted an obligatory kiss on Vanessa's forehead before taking a seat at the table.

"John, you've got to slow down. What's got you so hyper this morning?"

"Contracts coming due this week, the economy is shot, and you know we haven't had our best year. I'm a little tense about it, okay?"

A cell phone rendition of "We're in the Money" began to play somewhere in the house, and John pushed back his seat to search for his phone. He picked up his coat from the back of the couch, but the sound wasn't coming from there. As it started again, he turned toward the music to see his teenage daughter descending the stairs.

She answered the phone. "Welcome to Money Morning Madness, this is Mandy, how may I help you?"

John held out his hand, and his daughter offered up the phone and gave him a peck on the cheek as she passed him on the way to the table. "Morning, Dad."

If an employee had pulled such a stunt, John Money would have slapped the unfortunate miscreant with a pink slip faster than the Money Machine could walk past a Salvation Army red kettle without dropping in a single penny. For his daughters, his fuse was a little longer, but they were careful not to play with fire too often.

John lifted the phone to his ear. "This is John Money." He took a step toward the table and stopped. "What? Dixon is what? Paper? No...not that. What paper?" He motioned to Vanessa with one hand, but she couldn't tell what it was about. "Yes. You bet I'll take a look."

He snapped the phone closed. "Oh, this is just great. Where's the morning paper? Martha!"

Martha entered the room carrying a coffee pot in one hand and the paper under her arm.

John snatched the paper from Martha and dropped back into his chair. He frantically tore through the pages until he found the business section, dumped the rest on the floor, and scanned the section until he spotted a particular story on page 2. "Oh, great. Here it is... Donald Dixon to announce merger matters today. How can he do that?"

Martha placed a bowl of steaming oatmeal in front of John. As the smell of low-fat artificial cinnamon flavoring rose over the edge of the paper, John took a look at the goop. He grabbed a spoon, scooped up some lumpy goo, and let it drop back into the bowl. "Martha? What is this?"

She looked around the room. "The three-ring circus? Oh, you mean the breakfast?"

"This goop is breakfast? For whom? The three bears? Whatever happened to crispy maple-cured bacon, eggs over easy, and flaky buttermilk biscuits covered with black-pepper cream gravy? Now, that's what I call a man's breakfast."

Martha glanced at Vanessa for support.

"John. Get a grip," said John's wife. "We're not twenty years old anymore. We have to watch our cholesterol."

"How can I watch anything when the sight of this...this goop makes me nauseous?"

"At least give it a try. We'd like to keep you around for a few more years."

John handed the bowl back to Martha. "Try again, please."

John lifted the newspaper up, and Mandy poked at it. "Dad, can you pick me up after dance class today? Mom has a hair appointment and..."

John lowered the paper and stared at Mandy. "Excuse me? Can't you tell that I have monsters chomping at my back side? And you want me to take off because Mom needs a haircut?"

Vanessa mocked offense and talked to Mandy in a southern drawl. "Haircut? Dear me, no. Don't listen to him, Mandy. Men get haircuts. Women get hairdos. In fact, I think I'll do it up special today and go blonde, maybe platinum. Whatcha think, precious, should mommy go for it?"

Mandy mimicked her mother's accent. "Oh, dawlin...you no doubt will be the belle of the ball."

They both flashed toothy smiles at John.

John didn't smile back. "My professional life is hanging in the balance, and I'm living at Mel's Diner with Lula Bell and Bonnie Sue..."

"John...we're trying to get you to lighten up a little," said Vanessa. "You've been way too serious lately. It can't be good for you. You need to calm down before you have a heart attack."

"Calm down? You want me to calm down?"

"Yes. I want you to calm down. I'll pick Mandy up today. Now, does that help with the monsters?"

"Thank you, yes. And now, you can watch me calming down." John popped the paper back open and held it in front of him like a wall.

Martha reentered the room, carrying another bowl. She reached around John's *Dallas Morning News* and placed it on the table in front of him. John peered around the edge of the paper. He picked up a spoon and lifted up a scoop of granola cereal. He turned the spoon slightly and allowed the clumps of nuts and oats to tumble back into the bowl.

"Now, what is this?" he asked.

Martha shook a box of cereal. "It's the closest thing I could come to what you call breakfast."

"This is...kibbles and bits. Do I look like a West Highland white terrier to you? No offense, Mitzy."

Mitzy, previously oblivious to the goings on, perked up her ears.

Vanessa tried again. "It's low-fat natural-grain granola, John. And it's…"

Like anyone who's been married over twenty years, John finished the sentence. "…good for me. I know."

"…and helps you stay healthy."

"You want me to stay healthy! I tell you, I'm as healthy as a horse! And do you know why? It's because I feed on competition; I pounce on opportunity; I exercise my stock options daily. I'll be here long after the tofu generation's hit the showers."

"Cute. Very cute. Is that the best you can do?"

"On an empty stomach, yes…"

"John, it's only…"

"…that you love me, and I appreciate that."

"Yes."

"Then you'll understand why I need energy food to load up for today's battle."

"Carbs and calories, you call that energy food? It's artery-clogging, middle-age-murdering junk food. And that's the last thing you need."

"Okay, okay. I get it. And after today's storm passes, I'll hop back on the tofu train. Are you satisfied?"

"If you promise, cross your heart."

John crossed his heart, hearkening back to some youthful ritual. "And hope to die…"

"We just want to keep you around for a while," said Vanessa. "Mornings wouldn't be the same without your spry wit and shiny head."

"Yeah, Dad, you're not much to look at, but hey, you're all we've got."

John half-smiled at Mandy. "I love you too, precious." He then disappeared again behind the paper.

After a few bites of her own oatmeal, Mandy broke the silence. "So, Mom, is it okay if I sleep over at Morgan's tonight?"

"Tonight? I don't think so. It's a school night, and you know…"

"Dad, tell her it's okay. You have that PTA meeting, and Morgan and I need to work on that biology project."

Vanessa gasped. "The PTA! John, don't forget you promised to speak at the PTA meeting tonight. If you back out again, they'll wonder if Mandy really has a father."

John offered no acknowledgement.

"John... you are planning to speak tonight, right?"

Silence.

Vanessa tried again. "Hello, John?"

"Forget it, Mom. I think we wore him out. And now he's officially tuned out and in *the zone*. Earth to Dad, come in, please... He is so gone."

"In the zone?"

"Yeah, I don't think he can even hear what we're saying."

Martha came back to the room in time to hear Vanessa return to her southern persona. "Well then, it's time I confess. John, I appreciate your understanding my decision to leave you for the pool boy. I know it comes as a shock to you, especially after my series of rendezvous with the gardener, but I can no longer deny my love for the smell of chlorine."

Vanessa and Mandy laughed. Martha didn't get the joke.

"Right, Dad...you do remember that you said I could pierce my navel, shave my head like Britney did, and use the car to go camping this weekend with the football team, right?"

John lowered the paper, slowly, and peered over the top. "Funny, funny, funny. Very funny. First...I said I would speak to the PTA if I had time. I don't have time tonight, so I won't. Next, why not let Mandy go to Morgan's after dance class? You can get a fresh coat of platinum on your cranium and let the pool boy see it first. And I appreciate the heads-up on the gardener; it explains the pathetic landscaping this year. Now, if you'll excuse me, I need to escape this soap opera and get to my office where life is no joke." John pushed back his chair, grabbed his tie and briefcase, and headed for the door.

Vanessa stood to stop him, "John, you know we were just kidding. You're so tense every morning. Lighten up a little. Come on, you need something for breakfast. Remember the monsters?"

"I'll get a donut at the office."

"Dad? Does this mean I can shave my head, pierce my navel, and spend the weekend camping with the football team?"

"No problem...thirty minutes after I'm dead."

John closed the door behind him and Vanessa sighed. "That man is going to be the death of me."

Martha crossed her arms. "I bet he gets me first."

"Dad, wait a sec—you're leaving early this morning."

Chapter 3

The morning sun shone bright in the Texas sky over Dallas. The old oak tree that shaded the Money yard was alive with the enthusiastic rat-a-tat pecking of a redheaded woodpecker and the scurrying of two brown squirrels in love. The yard bore the signature of a landscaping company that had been well compensated to design and maintain the home's gardens. Pots of red begonias and white and pink periwinkles lined the Money sidewalk leading from the front door to the driveway, orange trumpet vines flowed down the stone wall like a waterfall, and a faint smell of sweet honeysuckle wafted through the air. Although the funds to support this picture-perfect garden spot came from the well-fed bank account of John A. Money, he saw, heard, and smelled none of it. He also didn't see his older daughter Kelly coming up the walkway to meet him until she almost bumped into him.

"Dad, wait a sec—you're leaving early this morning."

John's sour face turned into half a smile. "Ah, Kelly, my girl— The Mom and Mandy sitcom is in full force at the breakfast table. Enter at your own risk. Maybe you can knock some common sense into them."

Kelly kissed her dad on his bald head, as was the family custom. "But I wanted to talk to you both this morning."

John continued walking down the sidewalk toward his prized black Mercedes 550. "As much as I'd love that, it'll have to wait—trouble brewing at the office…call me later. We'll talk."

Kelly followed. "Just quick. Can I bring a friend home for dinner tonight?"

"Friend? Tonight? What friend? Do I know her?"

"Him. We've been on a couple of dates and…"

"Whoa. Bad timing, sweetheart…not tonight."

John opened the back door of the black Mercedes and put his brief case and coat on the leather backseat. He looked up at Kelly, and his entire body paused for a second, which was not a common occurrence in his ADHD world of perpetual motion. After his brain had processed this particular thought that had caught him off guard, his nerve endings fired up again, in all their sarcastic glory.

"Him? As in a person of the opposite you-know-what?"

"Yes, Dad. He is a boy. A male of the species."

"And he's a friend?"

"Yes."

"A friend who is a boy?"

"You've got it."

"A boy who is a friend?"

"Yes, Dad, he is a boyfriend. Is that what you're looking for?"

"A boyfriend where you have dates? What kind of dates?"

"You know, movies, concerts, church. Normal date stuff."

He closed the car's back door and crossed his arms. "I see. So what's this guy's name? Where's he from?"

"Austin."

"Is that where he's from or his name?"

"His name is Austin. He's from Denver."

"Denver from Austin?"

"Austin from Denver."

"Austin's a city, not a person. This guy already sounds confusing. I don't like confusing. I like straightforward. What's his major? Banking? Finance? Law? Premed?"

"Linguistics."

"Ling-what?"

"He studies languages. He's very brilliant at it."

John opened the driver's door and started to get in. "Languages? That sounds like a career that'll bring in the big bucks."

Kelly wedged herself between her dad and the car. "There's more to life than money, Dad."

John took a step back. "Um-hmm, you are exactly right, my dear. Let's see. There's food, clothes, houses, cars...hold on, all those take money. Hmm, back where we started. You can do better than some brainiac that studies words. Words are cheap. Find someone who studies gold. That's something solid. Now, if you'll excuse me..."

Kelly didn't move. "He wants to work in developing countries— you know, teach the illiterate how to read and write.

"I wish him the best. Believe me, let him go on his insane adventure. You'll be better off." John nudged Kelly out of the way and sat down in the driver's seat.

Kelly held the door open. "Dad! Stop for a second. Wait."

"Is there more here than you're telling me? Please don't tell me you're falling for this guy."

"No. I mean yes. I mean maybe. That's not the point."

John reached for the door handle, but Kelly stepped in front of it. "Then there is a point? Make it, please. I've got real work to do."

"There's a calling on my life."

"A what?"

"A calling. The Lord is calling me to the mission field."

"Okay, hold on." John fumbled for a word. "To what?"

"To work in Bible translation."

To Kelly's surprise, her dad got back out of the car and stood at his full height in front of her. "Bible translation? This is a career? Didn't we buy a Bible for Aunt Peggy last Christmas? And they had a King James, a New King James, an NI something...and something revised. And we really need more of them?"

"Not that type of translation, Dad."

"Get to the point. I don't have time for Bible games."

"I've studied all about the languages of the world and where translators are most needed. And I've prayed about it, and...I want to be a translator in the Tatar language."

"The Tay-teer language? Oh, yeah. That's the ticket to success. Sign me up for a two-pound baked tater with butter and sour cream. Is that what people speak in Idaho? Does it come with little packets of ketchup?"

"Everything is a joke with you."

"No, not everything. But this is."

"Why?"

"Why? I'll tell you...get a grip on reality. Reality is your hundred-thousand-dollar hallowed-halls college education. That's why."

Kelly knew this tone of voice. She crossed her arms as if to fend off the oncoming verbal attack.

"Maybe a hundred grand seems a pittance for someone bent on saving the world. But to a real working human, it's a lot of money. And I didn't spend that kind of money on your college experience so you could run off and write a Bible in some french fry language."

"Dad, why can't you..."

John pushed his way in to the car and sat back down in the driver's seat. "This conversation is over."

"No...it is not!"

"Okay, let's end with this! I'll make it simple. If you keep up with this stupid idea of yours, I will not pay your car payment, your fancy college tuition, or your sorority bills. If you're going to throw away your life chasing crazy dreams, don't expect me to be crazy enough to support it. Now, did you understand that language, or do I need to translate it into mashed potatoes?"

Kelly didn't know whether to cry or yell, so she did a little of both. "You wouldn't do that."

"Don't try me. Not today."

"But Dad…"

"End of conversation. I've got important work to do."

John reached around Kelly and grabbed the door handle and pulled on it, pushing her out of the way.

Kelly held the door open a few inches. "Why won't you listen?"

"I've heard every word. Maybe you should listen."

"I don't mean listen to me."

"Good..."

"I mean to Him." She looked heavenward.

John pushed her fingers from the door, and as he closed it, he said, "Have Him get on my calendar."

As soon as the door closed, John pushed the lock. Kelly pulled up on the door handle and nothing happened. The car started, and John flipped opened his cell phone and put it up to his ear, ignoring her. He put the car in gear and moved slowly down the driveway.

"Stop...Dad..."

As the Mercedes passed her, she banged on the window and then on the trunk until the car gathered enough speed to get away from her. As her dad drove down the street, Kelly buried her face in her hands and broke into tears.

***

Ricky Jenkins owned two business suits, both bought off-the-rack and on sale at JC Penney, one gray and one blue. When the blue one was at the cleaners, he wore the gray one, and when the gray one was at the cleaners, he wore the blue one. Each suit included one matching tie. Today was a blue suit and blue tie day. With his blue tie in his hand, he sat at the kitchen table with his young daughter Kaitlyn and son Noah while his wife Beth stood waiting for the toast to pop up. The first course in his breakfast consisted of two stacks of bills, ones that could be paid and ones that had to be postponed. He looked at Beth. "So, what's it gonna be?"

Beth buttered a piece of toast with the smallest tad of margarine possible and sliced it in half, giving one triangle to each of the children. "What do you mean?"

"Cell phone...or water? We can't pay both. You want to talk or take a bath?"

"We knew me staying home wouldn't be easy."

"Did we know it'd be impossible? We can't make it on my measly salary. Not with two kids. Something's got to give."

Beth sat down at the table and poured the orange juice. "God's never let us down. We need to keep praying. Things will turn around. I know it."

"Right...that's the ticket. Pray. Look around at this dump of an apartment It's easy to see that our prayers have worked well so far. It's like we're living in a royal palace."

"So, we're not rich in worldly things, but the Lord didn't bring us this far to drop us."

"Yeah... Now would be a good time."

Beth looked confused. "Excuse me?"

"We don't have too far to fall."

She reached over and kissed him on the cheek. "We're rich in what matters—I've got you and Kaitlyn and Noah. You'll see...God's watching out for us. We'll be fine."

"I wish I had your confidence."

Although Kaitlyn heard her name during the conversation, she was too busy playing with her father's tie. In her small, three-year-old mind, bill paying didn't rank high. What did rank high was the question about what would happen if the tie were stuffed into the half-empty orange juice glass. It would be like an experiment she'd seen done by the science guy on PBS.

Beth didn't notice the tie experiment in progress. "Now, get your tie on before— Oh, no!"

Ricky saw the experiment's result, grabbed the tie and held it up with orange juice dripping back into the glass. "This is all I need..." He looked at Kaitlyn with the intention of giving her a lesson in responsibility, but her blue eyes and angelic countenance melted the father's heart, as it always did. "Well, I guess I have no choice—it's my day to go tieless." Ricky stood up and grabbed his keys. He went around the table and gave everyone a kiss on the head. Kaitlyn was his last stop. "Squeeze all the juice out of that tie, young lady. I'll drink it tomorrow morning. We can't afford to waste anything."

"You're crazy, but I love you," said Beth as Ricky opened the door to exit. "You'll see. God's watching out for us."

***

The Lone Star Donut shop had been a Dallas institution since 1955. Over the years, millions of the round, sugary delicacies have been deep-fried at the historic donut factory and shipped in white boxes to schools, short order diners, and convenience stores all over Texas. Neighborly Dallasites, rich and poor alike, had come in droves every morning to satisfy cravings for glazed goodies and hot fresh coffee. A plaque on the store wall testified to the glory of the holed confection: "As you amble through life, brother, whatever your goal; keep your eye on the donut, and not on the hole."

A day ago, an unfortunate customer had passed away in his Naugahyde booth when he was visited by a short, stocky, and otherwise-invisible man wearing a flowery Hawaiian shirt. Affectionately known to his coworkers as A.D., the same man visited the store today. This time his goal was not to collect the soul of a customer. Instead, he stood in line at the counter with customers who would live to see another day. A.D. glanced over to the booth in the corner and gave thanks for the man who had introduced him to the pleasure of jelly-filled donuts.

While the stocky man waited his turn, John Money burst into the donut shop, bypassed the line, and walked up to the counter, tapping it with his keys. He pointed to the rack of glazed donuts and interrupted the saleslady in the middle of her transaction.

"I need a dozen of those donuts, pronto. Half glazed, half chocolate."

The cashier had waited on the occasional obnoxious customer for twenty-one years. Unlike the employees at John Money's office, this feisty little lady didn't cave in to Money's every whim. "Sir, you'll have to wait your turn." She pointed to the end of line.

John looked at the queue of people, quickly calculating eight people times one or two minutes each equals sixteen minutes. "My turn? Not likely."

He spun around and came face-to-face with an elderly woman who could reach five foot tall if she stood on her tiptoes. However, this lady was no pushover either. She raised a wrinkled finger into John's face. "Now, young man...watch your manners. If I were your mother, I'd..."

John stepped aside and kept going. "Yeah, well you're not my mother, thank God."

The man in the Hawaiian shirt shook his head. "Hurry, hurry, hurry. Why are some people always in a hurry?"

The cashier asked, "May I help you?"

The stocky man turned to the lady at the counter. "Absolutely." He pointed at one of the pastries. "What is that?"

"The éclair?"

"Oh, I like that sound. Eee-clair. Does it have stuff in it?"

"Yes, sir, custard."

"Okay, that sounds promising. I'll take two e-clairs."

The cashier bagged up the éclairs and set them on the counter. The man placed a twenty-dollar bill on the counter and turned to walk away.

"Sir, it's only $3.38. You forgot your change..."

The man looked back at the cashier with one éclair already in his hand. "Keep it."

"But, it's a twenty-dollar bill."

"Hey...you can't take it with you."

The cashier smiled. "This is a great day to be alive."

A.D. smiled back at her. "They all are, sister. They all are."

Outside the donut shop, the éclair customer glanced up at the sky as if looking for something. He took a clipboard from under his arm and looked at it while biting down on the pastry. "Okay...let's see." A glob of custard fell on the paper. "Oh, no you don't." He wiped off the goo and licked his finger as he tried to make out the names on the assignment sheet. "Okay, who was the guy in Dallas? Moo...Maa...Mee...Moe. Ah...oh yeah... Money, John A..." He glanced at his watch. "Hmm...a tad early...but not too. So, John A. Money in Dallas...why not let's you and me take a little trip together."

Chapter 4

Across from the Dallas Museum of Art in downtown Dallas stood a five-story building that houses Money Marketing Enterprises. For fifteen years, business owners in Dallas had come to MME for help promoting new stores, selling services and gizmos to the public, and making lots of good-old American cash. However, when the economy stumbled, the cash stopped coming in, and MME couldn't help the clients bring in new customers, these same business owners looked for greener pastures. And those instances put John A. Money into a bad mood. Such was the case this morning concerning his longtime client Donald Dixon.

At 7:59 the elevator doors opened on the fifth floor offices of MME. Ricky Jenkins, wearing his blue JC Penney suit, minus his blue tie, exited the elevator. He walked up to the receptionist, peered over her counter, and drummed his fingers. Two piercing eyes looked up at him over the top of a *Psychic Today* magazine.

Ricky knew the penalty for disturbing Marge in the middle of some important activity, and for Marge, the latest gossip in her favorite magazine was a celestially important activity. Ricky turned to leave before she'd have a chance to cast her mental darts into him. He was too late.

She slammed down the magazine. "Ricky. Stop. Don't move."

Ricky froze in his tracks.

"I'm getting something." She put her hands to her temples and closed her eyes. "Dry cleaners. That's it. You forgot to go to the dry cleaners to pick up your tie. Am I right?"

Ricky breathed. "Not exactly."

"Hmm, it's still early. Maybe I haven't had enough of my special celestial tea. It's very good, you know. Hardly ever fails to stimulate my cerebral cortex into psychic vibration, if you know what I mean.

Ricky didn't have a clue. "Wait. I can see something. You're going to ask Money for a raise today? Right? I mentioned that yesterday."

"So you are asking. And where is your tie?"

"Yes, and orange juice." Ricky noticed that Marge's lips had a purple hue to them. He didn't know if it was lipstick or if she was about ready to keel over and die. She didn't die. Instead, she took a deep breath, held it for a few seconds as if in great thought, then exhaled one long stream of air before she spoke again.

"You said orange juice? This is an important sign. Wait, yes, I see the carton in my mind. It's… orange. Yes? Organic with pulp? Pulp is good for you. Stimulates the reflex elasticity of the brain. What does it have to do with your tie?"

"Store brand, and it's a long story."

Marge pointed the sharp end of a pencil at Ricky. "I know your problem, Ricky. Trust me on this. You have to do more than just ask Mr. Money for a raise. You must bring the cosmos onto your side. It's an ancient secret. Listen and learn. You must imagine success. Imagine success in your mind, in the innermost folds of your brain, in the deep crevices of your existence. Imagine success, and success will find a way to your doorstep."

"It sounds a little weird to me."

"Shhh. Don't say that. Don't think that. It spoils the energy."

"What energy?"

"Cosmic."

"Comic? Cosmic. Cosmic. Listen to me."

"What?"

"Forget it."

"Besides, Beth says we need to keep praying, and then I'll get a raise."

"And do you have a raise?"

"Not yet."

"And how much is that new transmission for your van?"

"Seven hundred and fifty."

"Last month's doctor bills?"

"Three hundred."

Marge shook her head and rolled her eyes. "Forget prayer. What you really need is a mantra. It works every time. Here's what you do. Say to yourself, *I deserve a raise; I deserve a raise.* Say it with me."

Ricky reluctantly repeated it with her. "I deserve a raise. I deserve a raise."

"Keep it up, and this is what will happen—your spoken words will create a cosmic atmosphere to attract a raise. It's like a confluence of good vibrations. It will vibrate the raise toward you. Do you see? And if Money's in a good mood, you might actually have a chance."

At 8:07, the elevator door opened and Marge and Ricky heard the footsteps of John Money coming down the hall, across the tile floor.

Marge hid her copy of *Psychic Today* under a stack of other papers and looked busy. "Uh, those are not the footsteps of a happy man. Forget the mantra, better luck tomorrow."

Ricky hurried away from the counter before John arrived at the desk.

Marge smiled at her boss. "Good morning, Mr. Money, did you have a nice weekend?"

John barely acknowledged her. "Get Ricky and Howard in my office immediately. Plus every file on the Dixon deal...financials, advertising, staffing...everything... pronto! And hold all my calls." He turned and stomped into his office.

Marge stuck out her tongue toward Mr. Money's office, "Why, yes, Mister Money, I did have a nice weekend. I lost my spleen, my poodle ran off with a Chihuahua, and my boyfriend is in jail for drunk driving. Thanks for caring."

She picked up the phone receiver and punched in numbers with the tip of her elongated purple fingernail. "Ricky, the beast is alive and requesting an audience with you on the Dixon contract. Guess that makes you breakfast."

She punched in another number as she talked to herself. "Get me this; make me that....blah, blah, blah. Oh, is that you, Howard? The king is requesting P&Ls on Dixon and wants answers like yesterday."

Ricky arrived at Marge's desk with folders in hand by the time she hung up. "So you think he's in a bad mood?"

"If he's breathing, he's in a bad mood."

"I've still got to ask for that raise."

"The stars are not right, I'm telling you. There is no chance in the cosmos that you're getting anything from him today except grief."

Ricky swallowed hard. He crossed over to Money's office, stood for a second, glanced back at Marge, then knocked on the door and opened it a crack. John sat at one end of a table, files spread out before him. Ricky entered and stood at the other end of the table shifting the folders from one hand to the other. "You wanted to see me, sir?"

John looked up. "No, I could care less about seeing you. What I want is the status on the Dixon deal. Did you see the morning paper? Dixon's eyeing other agencies. Do you know what that means?

"Uh, status?"

"Am I alone here? Wake up, man. What are you getting paid for? Yes. Status, a noun...meaning, where are we?"

Ricky faked a laugh and took a step toward the table. "Well sir...the reality is..."

The door flew open, and Howard Richardson entered the room like a man on fire. He pushed his way past Ricky, took a seat next to John, and stared at his boss with a plastic smile. Immediately he started tapping on the table with his fingers, a testament to the twenty cups of coffee he'd consumed over the past few hours. He barely acknowledged Ricky, and turned to look at his boss. "So, you wanted to see me, big guy?"

Outside the office, on the balcony that ran the length of the picture window, the stocky man in the Hawaiian shirt, who was nibbling on the remains of a chocolate-covered pastry, peeked into the room and was somewhat amused at the goings-on. He didn't get to laugh much in his line of work, and this particular meeting looked like it might have some comic relief. As he walked back and forth on the ledge, observing the activity in the office, no one noticed him.

John backed away a few inches from Howard's invading stare. "Yes, Howard, Ricky and I were about to discuss the status on the Dixon deal. Bad news in the morning paper..."

Howard held up a red folder and waved it in the air. "Say no more, boss man. I saw the printed page and took action. I'm your action guy."

"According to this story..."

Howard's caffeinated muscles were twitching to get in on the action. He interrupted. "Come on, boss man. These know-nothing reporters are a bunch of wannabes planting some "confidential" poop and calling it a scoop. Pleeeezzeee, who could take this Dixon deal from us?" He slapped the red folder on the table, flipped it open, and pulled out a wad of papers, spreading them out before John. "Yes, sir, I burned the midnight oil. Did a pile of what-if spreadsheet scenarios while slurping down a dozen *venti* cups of Starbuck's best Arabica. But I dare say it was worth the lack of snooze time. I mean, check this out..." He twitched and gave Ricky a quick sarcastic wink.

On the balcony, the stocky man looked at a list on his clipboard and then looked at the nameplate on the desk, John A. Money. He smiled and stepped toward the window and through it. The inhabitants of the room felt a chill in the air, as if the air conditioning had just switched on. They all ignored it.

John looked over Howard's papers. "Good work, Richardson, I think..."

"...and you would be right, boss man. We can hold hands on that." He reached over and tugged playfully on John's tie. "Hey, nice neckwear, big kahuna... Armani? Burberry?"

"Thanks...it's actually..."

"No words needed, el capitán. Power tie for a power guy. I can dig it..."

The stocky man stood behind John. "Oh, this Money guy's got his own personal brownnoser. How special. Dig it deep, Richardson...then step in it, please. Your time will come soon."

No one in the room heard the stocky man's observation, but a chill ran up John's spine, and he turned and glanced behind him. He saw nothing.

Howard continued his caffeinated diatribe. "Fret not, dyno-dude. Dixon is done. *No problemo.* Now, some would say we should have seen it coming..."

John agreed, "Some would say..."

Howard continued, "...and they would be right. Frankly, we had a few less-than-spectacular quarters with this account in the past. But...with a little smoke and mirrors, a couple of pie charts, and a fancy slide show we can sail through this like a luxury liner on a clear day."

Ricky muttered under his voice, "More like the Titanic."

John looked up. "Excuse me?"

Ricky smiled. "I said...gigantic, this could be gigantic."

The telephone rang. John hit the speaker button. "Marge, I thought I said hold my calls!"

Marge's voice responded, "You'll want this one. David Dixon on one."

John hung up and motioned for silence. He cleared his throat and forced a smile. Howard gave him an energetic two thumbs up. The stocky man stood next to John, although no one saw him.

John picked up the phone. "David, good morning! What's the good word?"

After a brief silence, John's face did not display any happiness. "Come on, David. We've run the demographics on this deal. We're golden. We've got pie charts... I've got my, uh, best man working on this. Turnaround is in the air."

The stocky man smiled. "Pie charts? I like pie...chocolate?" No one heard him.

Howard glanced at Ricky, winked, and mouthed the words, "Best man!"

John's smile turned to a frown. "Hello...hello? David?" He removed the receiver from his ear, stared at it for a moment, and hung it up.

Howard leaned forward. "He's with us, right? The pie charts always do it. I bet he liked the pie charts."

"Wrong. He didn't like anything."

Howard stared into the air for a second until his caffeinated nerves gave him the spark of a new idea. "Plan B," he said, "It's coming to me. We gotta put our minds to it. There's always a plan B."

John stared out his window, right through the invisible stocky man. "I didn't build up this company by giving up. We just have to put our minds to it. There's always a plan B."

Howard had a quizzical look on his face. He turned to Ricky and muttered, "Didn't I just say that?"

John slammed a fist on his desk. "Get Phyllis with the financials. I don't go down without a fight. It's time to circle the wagons."

Howard stood. "Wagons. Circle. Right. John Wayne. Watch me run." He bolted out of the room.

Silence followed as John stared at the ceiling.

Ricky broke the silence. "Sir? What should I do?"

John never looked at Ricky. "You? What should you do? What should any of us do? Pray that we'll figure out plan B."

The stocky man nodded his head. "That's always effective. Maybe this dude's not so clueless after all."

Ricky dropped to his knees and folded his hands. "Dear Lord, I know Beth says you answer prayer, but..."

John looked at Ricky. "What are you doing?"

"Uh, I'm praying?"

"You, idiot. Get up off your knees. We need real solutions."

The stocky man folded his arms. "Hmm...bad call. You had something going there, Rick."

Ricky stood and wiped his pants' knees. "Kidding...of course. I knew that. Uh, sir. So? What do you want me to do?"

John reached into his wallet and pulled out twenty dollars and threw it onto the table. "Go get some donuts."

"Donuts?"

"Circular pastries, deep-fried in grease? Do I have to draw you a picture?"

"Yes, sir, I am aware of what they are."

"Then quit standing there like a fence post and go get them."

The stocky man's eyes lit up. "Finally, someone is making sound decisions. Grab me an éclair, Ricky, chocolate on the top with custard in the middle."

Ricky answered John, "Yes...sir."

After Ricky left the room, John slammed his fist into the table. "I am so dead."

The stocky man stood beside him "Soon and very soon..."

Always a bit curious about the life lived by his clients, the stocky man walked around the office. He found a plaque on John's desk and read it to himself. "John A. Money, a Success, Whatever the Cost." He next spotted a candy dish and looked to see if John was watching, remembering that there are rules that governed his activities. Of course, who could blame him if he sometimes fudged the rules a little, and in this case, he knew that John would never miss the morsel. Convinced that John wasn't looking, the stocky man took one of the candies, unwrapped it, and bit into it. "Mmm...chocolate. What a great day this is. First I discover donut éclairs, and now these chocolate thingies. I love my job." He grabbed a couple more candies and put them in his pocket.

John stood and looked out his window. "Idiots...I am surrounded by idiots."

The stocky man appeared at the other end of the room. "And a fine example to them all you are. But time's up, and I have other clients to visit, so let's end this visit with that profound thought." He made a motion toward John with his hand. John's hand went up to his chest as if he had lost his breath, but before Lucky could flick his wrist, Howard burst back into the office, followed by the company's middle-aged bean counter, Phyllis.

The stocky man lowered his hand, and John exhaled. "On the other hand, this could be fun to watch."

John shook off the feeling and returned to his seat. Phyllis and Howard sat across from their boss. He stared at them for a moment before he broke the silence. "Hello, people! What am I paying you for? Do you realize that our ship is about to sink? Gurgle, gurgle. Do you hear it? We're taking on water. Now...who has a plan?"

Howard flashed his million-dollar smile. "Now, Mister Money...you be Ginger Rogers and I'll be Fred Astaire, and we can..."

John exploded. "No more dance lessons, Howard. No pie charts, no smoke and mirrors. I need real answers."

Phyllis held up her hand. "If I may?"

John nodded, hopeful. "Yes, Phyllis, please."

"Well, sir, to the untrained eye..."

John pounded his fist on the table. "To the what?"

Phyllis repeated herself. "To the untrained eye..."

"Are you serious? I could care less about the untrained eye. We need twenty-twenty vision to shed some light on this train wreck. A plan, a clue, an answer. Do either of you have any real ideas?"

Ricky entered the office carrying a box of donuts. He dropped them onto the table and pulled open the lid.

Howard salivated., "All right, sustenance." He grabbed a chocolate-covered one. "This is what I mean. The perfect combination of sugar and chocolate."

Phyllis joined in, selecting a blueberry cake donut. "Blueberry. My favorite. I used to get one every Saturday morning before my grandfather and I went fishing."

John moaned.

The stocky man peered over Phyllis's shoulder with wide-eyed anticipation. "What? No éclairs? Bummer. You failed me, Rick."

John stared at them. "As soon as you're all finished loading up at the buffet, I would appreciate a plan. Any plan."

Howard swallowed the last bite of his chocolate delight, looked in the box again, and selected a fat confection. "All right. Jelly filled."

John screamed and waved his hands. "I'm dying here!"

Howard, donut hanging out of his mouth, looked up at his boss.

The stocky man threw up his hands. "Indeed you are, John A. Money! Indeed you are." He looked heavenward. "Open his eyes...so I can shut them."

"Circular pastries, deep-fried in grease? Do I have to draw a picture?"

Chapter 5

Seen only by John, a blast of blue smoke and a bright light flashed in the room. John almost had a heart attack. He closed his eyes, opened them again, and for the first time, he saw a stocky man in a Hawaiian shirt standing behind Phyllis.

"What the... What... Did you see that? How did you get in here? Who do you think you are?"

Phyllis stammered and almost burst into tears. "I'm Phyllis, sir. Don't you know me? Phyllis Tomkins from Accounting? You sent for me. I came in with Howard."

John pointed to the man behind Phyllis. "Not you, you, idiot. You."

Howard, Ricky, and Phyllis looked around the office and saw no one.

The stocky man laughed. "You know for an alleged big shot, you have a lot more powder than punch. This is the part of my job I like most, although the bigwigs say it's not the most professional way to approach the task. I mean, how often does someone in my line of work get to have a little fun?"

"Howard! Remove that idiot!"

Howard jumped to his feet and looked back and forth to Phyllis and Ricky. "Yes, sir... Which idiot, sir?"

The stocky man waved his hand in front of Howard's face. "Haven't you guessed? They can't see me."

"What? Who can't see you?"

"Them. They can't see me."

"Them?"

"Yes, them. Your underlings, your flunkies, your minions."

John looked at his minions for help. "Who can see this man?"

The three flunkies looked around the room and at each other. The stocky man vanished into thin air, leaving only a puff of blue smoke in his place.

"He's gone," said John.

Suddenly the vanishing man reappeared next to John.

"He's back."

The stocky man put a hand on John's shoulder. "This is between you and me. I'm thinking maybe they should go."

John flinched and backed away. "The only one going is you! Howard, do something!"

"Sir?"

The vaporous man vanished and reappeared behind Ricky.

John pointed. "Howard, are you telling me you can't see the man standing behind Ricky?"

Howard jerked around and turned toward Ricky but saw no man. "Behind Ricky? Which Ricky?"

"There. Right there. In the loud Hawaiian shirt."

The stocky man looked offended. "Loud? What's loud about this shirt?" He turned to show his profile. "Does it make me look fat? Doesn't it remind you of paradise? Maybe you'll wind up there."

"I'm not going anywhere. I've had enough of this. Now get out of here or I'll call security. I'm finished with you."

"Nice try. Wrong on both counts. We're not finished yet. This is just too much fun." The stocky man blew a kiss toward Howard.

"Howard, did you see it? He just blew you a kiss! You had to see that."

Howard looked where John was pointing into thin air. "Sir, this Dixon deal has you a little wound up. Maybe I should..."

"Maybe you should shut up and remove that idiot!"

The unseen visitor appeared beside John again. "You're digging quite a hole here, pal. The only idiot they see is you. Send the prisoners back to their dungeons. You and I need some quality time."

John looked at his watch. "Time? I'm a business man. I have no time."

The stocky man looked at his pickup list. "You still got a little." He suddenly appeared behind Ricky again.

John turned and looked at the stranger. "Okay...I'll make it simple. Who are you, and who are you with?"

Ricky gulped. "Ricky, sir...Ricky. You know, Ricky Jenkins with Marketing?"

"Not you, moron, him!"

Ricky looked behind him and all around. "Him, who...sir?"

The stocky man shook his head. "Send them away. You're beginning to look like a doofus."

John looked toward Ricky. "Doofus! Who are you calling a doofus?"

Ricky held up his hands. "No one. No, sir, no doofus. I never called anyone a doofus."

John fell into his chair with his head in his hands. "That's it...get out! Everyone!" He looked up and saw that no one had moved. "Have you gone deaf as well as blind? I said out!"

Howard spoke softly. "Mr. Money, I really think..."

John stared at him. "Not now, Howard. Just leave me alone. Go!"

The three workers picked up their papers and slipped out of the room. The stocky man followed them to the door. "Right, learn to think on your own time, Howie. And Ricky, keep praying. It couldn't hurt. And, oh yeah, Phyllis, I'm just saying, get a new hair stylist."

The door closed behind them, and the stocky man pulled up a chair next to John. "Whew...you wear me out! Is everything this tough with you?"

John stared at the visitor and shook his head. "I've gone nuts. It's the biggest disaster day in my history, and I'm talking to someone no one can see. Next thing you know, I'll be in a nursing home with a blanket on my knees muttering to myself. Wait, I'm already muttering to myself."

"You know, John, this doesn't have to be this hard."

"This? What is this? I have no idea what 'this' is."

The stocky man paced around the room. "Wow, no clue, have you?"

"No."

"You want to know what this is about?"

"No. I want you out of here."

"Not happening."

"Okay. I'm off my rocker. I get it. I'll play the game. What is this?"

"Now, you're talking."

"I'm listening."

"John, this is all about you. Y-O-U."

"Me?"

"Your life, the roads you've traveled, the sum of your collected parts. The final page of your journey. It's all about you. Now do you understand?"

John stared at the stranger. "Who are you?"

The stocky man crossed his arms. "Okay, then, enough about you. Let's talk about me."

"As I said, who are you?"

"Okay, then. I'm a little more complicated, John."

"Try me."

The stocky man strolled around the room. "I'm known by many names. Man at the End of the Road, the Crossing Guard, Captain Sunshine, the Great Reckoner."

John started to get it. "Wait a minute."

"Some call me Doctor Doom. Pale Rider. Jaws of Death."

"Wait, not the…"

"More often than not, I'm called, and I know you've heard this one…I can tell it's on the tip of your tongue."

"Grim Reaper?"

"John, I'm impressed. You're a quick study. Good job, yes...you're right on target. But, truth is, I hate that name."

"Wait. You're trying to get me to believe that you really *are* the Grim Reaper?"

The stocky man threw up his arms. "Okay, sure. Go with the obvious. But try to find something good in that name. How would you like to be called Grim? That'll get you on everyone's guest list. Let's invite Grim—he's good for a few laughs."

John shook his head in disbelief.

"John...do you want to know something?"

"Not really."

"I'll tell you. For the record, the name Grim Reaper is not my idea of coolness. Why did I get stuck with such a name? After all, what's wrong with my given name?"

"And that is?"

The visitor's eyes lit up, and he smiled. "Angel of Death. See how that rolls off the tongue. Angel of Death. I mean...Angel, that's a good thing. Kind of takes the edge off the dying part, huh?"

"No."

"Oh well, if that's a problem, you can call me Lucky."

"Lucky?"

"I like it."

"Why Lucky?"

"Why not?"

"No. I mean, wait. This is not happening." John picked up the phone, pressed a few digits, and spoke with a hint of desperation in his voice. "Marge? Are you there?"

Lucky smiled. "She can't hear you. The phone is, how can I say it? Dead. Quite dead."

John jumped up and lunged toward the door. He grabbed the knob but couldn't get it to open.

"No need to try the door. Dead...bolt."

John reached into his pocket and pulled out his cell phone and started punching numbers.

As he dialed, Lucky cut his hand across his throat and said in a mobster voice, "Your contract... has expired."

John stumbled back to his chair and sat down. "But, but, but...I don't get it."

"Call it a gift."

"No, I mean...I mean I don't understand this whole thing. Like, why me, why now? This cannot be happening to me."

Lucky stood next to John. "Yes, it is a true shame it had to happen right now. That whole Dixon deal was starting to make sense to even me."

"Dixon? I could care less about Dixon. I mean, I have things to do. Don't you understand? I have a wife. I have a family. We have things to do, places to go, memories to make. I mean, I don't even remember if I told them I love them this morning."

Lucky shook his head. "Bummer."

John picked up the phone and double clicked the switch hook. Lucky shook his head.

"Still dead."

John leaned back in his chair, closed his eyes, and placed his fingers on his temples.

Lucky wrinkled his brow. "What exactly are you doing?"

"Focusing on good energy. This is not happening. It's all because I skipped breakfast. You are nothing but a low-blood-sugar illusion. I must focus."

While John focused, Lucky took another chocolate candy from the dish and ate it. He stood directly in front of John with his face inches from John's.

John opened his eyes. "And when I open my eyes." John shrieked.

Lucky smiled. "Hi, there." While John pushed back his chair, Lucky held up a candy wrapper. "Say John, what are these?"

John tried to catch his breath. "You scared the life out of me!"

"Hey, it's my job."

"Let me think. Wait. I know. There's been some mistake."

"Here we go."

"No, now wait a minute."

"Save your wind, pal. I have walked this road a few times."

"I just know that there's some kind of goof here."

"Right, and that goof is named John A. Money."

"Come on, do I look dead to you?"

"Not quite yet."

"And you know why—because I'm not dead. First of all..."

"Wait. I know this one...you're too young."

"Yes!"

"And you've got too much to do."

"Absolutely!"

"Listen, John. You're never too young, and what needs to be done is done."

"So, that's it? I have no say? You swoop down here, eat my truffles..."

Lucky looked at the candy wrapper. "Truffles? Is that what they are? Very nice. I even like the name. Truff-les. Fun to say, don't you think?"

"No."

"I like it. Truff-les."

"Stop that."

"Okay then, have it your way. Are you ready?"

"Wait. No. There's got to be more to this. You're just going to drag me off to heaven, and I get no vote."

"Democracy, huh? Yes, I've heard of it. And because of that, you want a vote?"

"I think I deserve one."

"Okay, John, no one can say I don't have a little leeway here and there. You go ahead and vote."

"I vote that I should live."

"Very nice. I would have predicted that. Now, it's my turn. I vote that you should die." Lucky faked shock. "Oh, no. A tie! Let's go to the tiebreaker right here on my bona fide official clipboard." Lucky raised his list. "Yep, I was right. You made the list. You die! There, you voted. Feel better? No need to pack any bags. You can't take them with you, you know."

"So, I'm supposed to get up now and follow you to paradise?"

Lucky shrugged. "Well, now, don't get me wrong. I'm not going to mislead you. We go to the gate at least."

"Gate, what gate?"

"You've heard of them, I'm sure. The pearly ones. Long lines, cloud cover. Happy people with smiles, and some...with long, sad frowns. Come on, you know what I mean...THE GATE?"

John turned a pale shade of panic and swallowed hard. "Okay, yes, I've heard of those gates all my life. But, but I always thought they led to heaven. At least tell me that I'm going to heaven."

Lucky shrugged.

"You don't mean..." He swallowed hard again. "Hell?"

"Heaven or Hell. It's not for me to say. No, no, that's not in my job description. That's a question for Shipping."

"Shipping?"

"That's what I said. Receiving and Processing, that's me. I get you to the gate, then you're on your own."

"You're telling me that you don't know?"

"Do I have to spell it out? Yes, I'm telling you that's not my line. I don't have a clue. Now, are you ready?"

"No! Wait! I need to know! What can I do?"

"Little late for that, pal. Travel plans have been made; your ticket's been punched. It's a simple plan, really. Even you should be able to understand it. We get to the gate, they check the big book and...and you take the ride." He pointed up. "One way..." And then down. "...or another."

"Ride...what ride?"

"Think man, this is no jigsaw puzzle. You lived a life. You did what you wanted. You had your chance. You made your choice. That tells the tale."

The cell phone in John's pocket rang. Both men jumped, and John put his hand to his chest.

Lucky looked confused and scratched his head. "I thought I killed that."

It rang again.

Lucky pointed to John's pocket. "You gonna get it? It might be important."

John opened his coat and retrieved the phone. He punched a button and held it to his ear. "Hello?" He jumped back and held the phone out to Lucky. "It's for you."

Lucky took the phone. "You can run but you cannot hide." He put the phone to his ear.

"Yo, Lucky here. You got it...I'll...right, but like we discussed when in the... I know, I know...we did say... So...how soon is too soon? I need parameters here. Six? Twelve? What? Okay...you wear the suit, so you make the call." He closed the phone and handed it back to John. "Some folks can make eternity seem like forever."

John stood stiff, his eyes closed. "Okay...I'm ready."

"You are?" asked Lucky.

John opened his eyes. "But first, we do the show, right?"

"Show? What show? There's a show?"

"I know the drill. My life passes before my eyes? Okay, I'm ready. Let's get on with it."

"There is no show."

"What do you mean?"

"Just what I said. There is no show. Why does everyone want some kind of Technicolor presentation? I've heard it before. 'Oh, show me when I was four; that was a fun year. When I was seventeen I met Myrtle and she changed my world. I want to see that.' There is no show!"

"No flashing before my eyes?"

"You lived your life—you didn't make a movie. You want to remember? Remember on your own time."

"Of which I now have none."

Lucky shuffled his feet. "Well, now you've got me over a barrel. You've got a little."

"A little what?"

"Remember the phone call?"

"You mean…"

"I mean…"

"I'm not?"

"No, you are."

"So, I'm dying."

"Everyone dies. Otherwise I'd be without a job. But for you, not today."

A tentative smile broke out on John's face. "Oh, that's great. That's great…"

"Tomorrow…"

The smile vanished. "Oh, that's not so great."

"You got twenty-four."

"Twenty-four?"

"As in a day. Twenty-four hours. Listen, John, I was in the neighborhood, thought I'd cut down on some fly time. But the gate keepers have a problem if too many are brought in early. So, your T.O.D. is 0948 Tuesday. Got it? So, with that…I gotta fly."

"What is a T.O.D.?"

"Time of death."

"So, I am still gonna?"

"Oh, yeah. Hey, you got a day."

"But what do I do?"

"Again with the questions. No answers here, sport. Why not make it a day to remember?"

Lucky grabbed a few truffles out of the candy bowl. "John, one thing you can do."

"Yeah?"

Lucky popped a truffle in his mouth. "Get some more of these. Nice." Lucky took a bite out of a second truffle, and vanished.

"Ok, I'm ready"

Chapter 6

Howard crouched down by John's office with his right ear pressed up against the door. He contorted his mouth as if that helped him listen and stuck a finger in his other ear.

Marge came around from her desk and tried to peek through a slit in the blinds that covered the office window. "What's he saying?"

Howard put his left finger to his lips. "Shhh." He smelled his finger, said, "Ugh," and wiped it on his trouser leg.

Ricky paced in the hallway. "I hope we don't lose our jobs over this. I can't afford to lose my job. I have two kids, a wife, and an apartment to support."

Phyllis leaned against the opposite wall and wrote some figures on a legal pad with a number 2 pencil. "Let's see. If we end up losing the Dixon deal, that accounts for 12.2 percent of our gross income—at least from last year. There are twenty-three employees, and income last year was $1.7 million. I think if we could cut some of the ads to TV and radio stations and sell the box seats at the stadium, we could make up for the loss."

Howard looked at Phyllis. "Be quiet. He's talking to someone. I don't hear any answers. Something about the Grim Reaper."

"Grim Reaper? That doesn't sound good for our jobs," said Ricky.

Marge looked over the counter to the telephone bank. "He's not talking on the office phones. I think he's having an out-of-body experience."

Howard held up his hand. "Wait. He stopped talking. I can't hear what he's doing."

"You don't think he'll do anything dangerous?" asked Ricky. "Should we call 911?"

Phyllis wrote a figure down on her paper. "He does have a $2.5 million life insurance policy. But they don't usually pay for suicides."

Marge stepped back to her desk. "Get away from the door. If he comes through and sees you, you're all toast."

Howard stood up, stepped away from the door, and joined Ricky and Phyllis at the coffee pot on the other side of the lobby. They stared at the door for ten minutes as Howard consumed his twenty-first and twenty-second cups of coffee for the day. "I wish I had one of those chocolate-covered donuts," he said.

After fifteen minutes of staring at the door, Marge's phone rang. "It's him," she whispered to the group.

"Hello, Mr. Money. Everything okay? Yes. Yes. Yes, she's here. I'll send her in." Marge looked at the group. "Phyllis, you win the prize. He is requesting your presence."

Phyllis gathered up her file folders, stuck the number 2 pencil behind her ear, stepped up to John's office door, and opened it. "You...you wanted to see me, Mr. Money?"

John sat at his desk holding and staring at a picture of his family. He lifted his hand and motioned to Phyllis, never looking at her. "Yes, come in, Phyllis."

Phyllis came in, pulled out a seat by the table, sat down, and arranged her files on the table, the legal pad containing her latest hen-scratched calculations on top.

John never took his eyes off the family picture. "Please, Phyllis, take a seat."

Phyllis stood again and reseated herself, this time making more noise. "Thank you, sir."

John didn't respond. Phyllis shuffled her files, marked a few numbers on one of the pages, and sat in silence for a minute. Finally, she coughed. "You know, Mr. Money, I may have an idea on the Dixon deal." She held a page filled with columns of numbers. "If you look at the gross operating expenses over the last year..." She paused to see if he was listening.

John put the picture down and stared into Phyllis's eyes, making her squirm in her chair.

"You see, Mr. Money, I'm convinced if we turn from operating full time and focus on the tourist season, we can no doubt impact the Dixon bottom line."

John continued to stare at her. After a moment he spoke. "Phyllis, do you like me?"

Phyllis pushed the chair back a few inches. "Excuse me?"

"Do you like me?"

She smiled awkwardly and looked toward the door to see how far away it was in case she had to bolt for it. "Uh, sure...I mean..."

"What do you think of me?"

"Well, uh...now that's a tough one. I mean it's hard sometimes to verbalize correctly what I feel as it relates to the actual use of the word...think. I mean we sometimes think we know how we feel... I mean...what do you mean, when you say 'think'?"

John leaned forward, and Phyllis responded by leaning backward.

"Okay, Phyllis, let's try this. If someone were to say to you 'Tell me about John Money,' what would you say?"

"Oh, that...well."

"I'm a good man?"

"Uh, okay."

"I'm a good friend?"

"Uh, sure."

"A good businessman?"

Phyllis looked relived. "Yes, yes sir. We have a winner! Dead on...a good businessman. Now, that you are. I would have no trouble going along with that."

John hesitated. "A man bound for heaven when he dies?"

Phyllis's jaw fell open as she searched for a response. "Well…uh, okay…I guess. I mean…why not?"

John smiled and took a deep breath. "Exactly…why not? I'm a good guy. It's not like I beat my wife or cheat on my taxes."

Phyllis frowned.

"Well, I don't beat my wife."

She smiled in agreement.

"Thank you, Phyllis. I am humbled by your kind words."

"Yes, of course, Mr. Money."

"Good, good. You've made my day. You can go now."

"So…is that all? And, Dixon?"

"Who is Dixon? That's all, Phyllis. Good-bye. I'm a good guy, you know."

"I see. Yes, yes. Of course, thank you, Mr. Money."

As the door shut behind Phyllis, John sat back in his chair. "A good guy, yes…that's what I am. Heaven for me? Phyllis said it…why not? I know how to be a good guy."

"I'm a good man?"

Chapter 7

John called Ricky into his office and had him sit at the table. Ricky noticed something odd in his boss's eyes. He hoped it wasn't the look of someone about to fire him.

"Uh, Mr. Money, I realize it looked a little rough earlier, sir. But I really feel if we take a look at the demographics, we can be on our way to understanding this Dixon dilemma."

John stared at Ricky. "How long have you worked for me, son?"

Ricky glanced at his folder, looking for the answer before it soaked in that the question had nothing to do with Dixon. He wondered if this was going to be a good time to ask for a raise. "Five and a half years, sir."

"Like your job?"

"Oh, yes, sir, love my job. And about that..."

"Married?"

Ricky nodded.

"Kids?"

"Two."

John smiled. "Me, too. Two girls."

Ricky returned the smile. Maybe now that they were talking about family would be a good time to see about the raise. Before Ricky could get up the nerve to ask, John spoke again.

"Tell me something...how much do I pay you?"

"Thirty-two five, sir." *Was he going to fire me or cut my salary?* Ricky wondered.

"Mm, call me Scrooge," said John.

"Excuse me?" *Did he say Scrooge, or you're a boob?* Ricky asked himself.

"Nothing... And you have a house?"

"Not yet. I hope to someday. Right now we have a little two-bedroom apartment." He thought to himself, *That is until I get fired, then I'll be living on the street—or with Beth's mother. Please don't let that happen,* Ricky prayed.

"What kind of car do you drive?"

"A 1979 VW bus. Used to be my parents'. They sorta gave it to me when my Geo Metro died last year. I can't complain. It runs...most of the time." *Is he going to take that, too?* Ricky wondered.

John stood, and Ricky could see that he was in great thought. He prepared himself for the blow. *"You're fired!"* He could hear the voice of his boss in his mind. Maybe he would be kinder and say, "We'll work with an employment agency to help you." No, Ricky decided that John Money was more of the get-it-over with type. He held his breath.

"Give me the keys to your car," said John.

"But how am I going to pay the rent... What? Pardon me? My car?"

"Your car keys, can I see them?"

Ricky fished his keys out of his pocket and handed them over.

John pulled another set of keys out of a desk drawer. He dangled them in front of Ricky for a moment and then dropped them into his hands.

Ricky stared at them. "What's this?"

"Your new car."

Ricky examined the keys. "No, these are the keys to a Mercedes. Your Mercedes?"

John smiled. "Your Mercedes."

"My Mercedes?"

"Rated high in safety features. Important for a man to protect his family. We'll call it a trade."

Ricky's heart pounded in his chest, "M….M…More like a miracle… You okay, sir?" *We were right, he's crazy as a loon,* Ricky thought. *But who cares, now that he's giving away his Mercedes.*

John talked in a fatherly tone. "Yes, yes, Ricky. You see, this is the kind of thing good people do for each other. That's the kind of person I am."

"B…B…But I don't know what to say."

"Thanks is always nice."

"Yes, sir. Thanks!" *I wonder if Beth was praying for this?*

After a momentary silence, John put a hand on Ricky's shoulder. "Tell me something, Ricky."

"Anything…"

"You believe in God?"

Ricky tossed the keys in the air. "Do now!"

John faked a laugh. "Seriously. Do you believe in stuff like heaven?"

"Uh, sure…" *Is he going to ask me to give the keys back? Is this a test?*

"Think you'll go there?"

Ricky held up the keys. "Yes, sir. Pretty close right now."

John's face turned oddly serious. "And good people are the ones that go to heaven?"

Ricky was willing to agree to anything to keep the Mercedes. "Yes, sir. Good people…they go to heaven." *Did I say what he wanted to hear? I hope he doesn't ask for the keys back.*

"Then that seems to be the consensus. And…what about a good guy like me?"

"What? You, sir?"

"In heaven, I mean. Me?"

Ricky looked at the Mercedes keys in his hand. "Come on, a generous guy like you? As they say, God loves everyone."

John smiled and thrust out his hand. Ricky took it, and they shook. *That makes it a real deal, doesn't it? We shook hands on it.*

"Yes, yes, very good then, Ricky. You can go now. It was a pleasure being able to do a good deed for you. Remember that next time you and, what's her name?"

"Beth?"

"Yes, when you and Beth pray. Oh, and ask Marge to step in, please."

Ricky nodded his head, almost bowing to his boss as he picked up his folders and approached the door. When he opened it, Howard suddenly stood up, turned away, and slipped around the corner.

Ricky exited the office, rear first, making sure his boss wasn't going to suddenly ask for the keys. As soon as he was out, he closed the door and took a deep breath.

Marge put down her copy of the *New Age Reporter*. "Did he give you a raise?"

Ricky stepped over to the receptionist's desk and leaned on the waist-high shelf and flashed a big smile. "Not exactly...but I got his Mercedes...how great is that?"

"You got his Mercedes? Very nice."

"I can't believe it. It's like I'm rich or something..."

Marge fumbled with some papers. "Not to burst your bubble, sweetheart, but do you know how much the insurance is on that monster? I've been paying the bills on it. It ain't cheap. And the sucker uses premium gas. It's a guzzler, I tell you. Gulp. Gulp. Gulp. That's what it does. Gulps liquid gold. Now, how's that going to pay the doctor's bill? Just saying..."

"I hadn't thought about that." Ricky's smile disappeared as he caressed the indentations along the edge of the key and thought about how much each indentation was going to cost him. "Oh, yeah, he said he wants to see you next..."

"Yang more and ying less."

Chapter 8

Marge Carter played receptionist by day. She got the job at Money Marketing by hiring on as a temp and staying around long enough to become full-time. It didn't take a lot of skill, and it allowed her to read psychic magazines and play on YouTube most of the day. At night she lived another persona known as "Celeste de Venus," palm reader at a swank downtown nightclub. When she wasn't reading lines on people's hands, she told fortunes on the phone for $3.95 a minute. As resident soothsayer at Money Marketing, she practiced her skills by analyzing everyone's personal life situations, whether they liked it or not. After all, she'd been engaged six times and married three times by the time she was twenty-nine. She knew all the angles and transitioned from Marge's straight talk to Celeste's psychobabble in the blink of her pierced eyebrow.

When Mr. Money called her into his office, Marge/Celeste was never more ready to verbalize her opinion on the boss's personal dilemma. She sauntered into John's office like the Queen of Sheba, nestled into a chair, and listened to his whining about the afterlife. Celeste placed two fingers on either side of her head, looked up to the ceiling, and spoke in a ghostly whisper. "Mr. Money, Mr. Money, I can see in my spirit that you are carrying a heavy burden about the unknown. I see these spiritual concerns in my mind. I am in touch with the infinite, and together we can help you comprehend your spirit's significance in the vastness of the universe."

"Really?"

Marge turned her eyes toward her boss and dropped her hands into her lap. "But first off, personally, I gotta tell you. I'm not totally convinced about this whole heaven deal. It's overrated."

John looked startled. "What?"

"You want straight talk?"

"Of course"

"About heaven?"

"Yes, I want to know about heaven."

"Okay. Here's the deal," said Marge. "I mean, we're told it's there and when we die, no doubt, we pray it's there. But let's be real. As far as I can tell, no one has really been there and come back with a report on the validity of the claim. Is that right?"

John mulled over the question for a moment. "I see...so you are..."

Marge didn't let him finish. "I mean, for all we know this whole heaven thing could just be a marketing plan to sell books."

"Books? Books? You're saying heaven is a marketing invention created to sell...Bibles?"

"Bibles, smibles. I'm not saying it was and not saying it wasn't. I'm just saying think about it. Know anyone that has been to heaven and come back with photos?"

"Well…no."

Marge clapped her hands together. "So, there you go. But to answer your original question..."

"My original question? What was my original question?"

"You asked me if I think you'll go to heaven."

"So, you think there's a heaven for a guy like me?"

She wrinkled her pierced eyebrows. "Let's ask heaven, shall we? Are you listening? Can you hear the ether speaking? Listen. A word is coming. Yes. You must know this, there is more to the spiritual cosmos than you may be aware of."

"What spiritual cosmos?"

"You call it religion. You seek religion. I can sense it. But you limit yourself. There is not one religion, there are many religions. They must be synthesized. All spiritual beliefs lead to the truth if you open your mind to them."

"All of the beliefs?" asked John.

"Yes, eastern, western, ancient, and modern. You've got to study the stars as well as the grass and the bees."

"The bees?"

"Yes, especially the bees. They make the honey of life."

"They sting, too."

"They are the most balanced form of life's karma. We must learn from their balance. I can tell you this; if there is a place called heaven, the people who go there must live in harmony with nature like the bees—they must live in a balance between their yin and yang."

"Their yin?"

"And yang."

"And yang?"

"The two sides of life. The two energies of natural existence. I see in your life an overabundance of yin."

"And my yang?"

"Yes...you need more yang."

"More yang?"

"Exactly. You must balance your existence—learn to yang more, and yin less."

"Yang more?"

"And yin less. I think you're getting it."

Celeste looked content. John looked confused.

The office mystic continued, "Mr. Money, have you ever investigated your past lives to evaluate your karma?"

John shook his head. "No."

"I didn't think so. Here is what I see in my eye of eyes—and I can tell you this: I usually charge big bucks for this kind of insight..." She adjusted herself in her chair and leaned forward ever so slightly.

"Go ahead," said John.

"Here is what I see. If you purge your spirit of negative yin and reaffirm your positive yang toward your employees, for example give everyone raises, then the resulting karma would illuminate a celestial pathway to the eternal city. Don't you think?"

Chapter 9

John left his office and headed toward the coffee station, still pondering his yin and yang. Howard raced ahead of his boss, poured coffee in Money's favorite mug, and presented it to him.

"Thanks," said John, accepting the cup.

"All for a good cause," said Howard as he stirred his own coffee in rapid swirls. "So," said Howard, "Interesting day? What's up, big boss?"

John held the warm cup in his hand. "Heaven," he said.

"I'm for it," said Howard. "Who couldn't like heaven? It's a great place. Heavenly."

"Have you ever thought about going there? Heaven, I mean?" asked John.

"Sign me up," said Howard.

"Phyllis says good people go to heaven."

"And right she is. Good people, that's the ticket," said Howard.

"Yeah, good people. That's what they say. So, Howard, what do you think about me?"

"You? Mr. Great Boss himself? Yes, sir. Businessman like no other. Look at this place, your baby, your brainchild. How good is that?"

"I mean good like what it takes to get to heaven. I'm wondering if I'll go to heaven." John headed down the hall toward his office.

Howard followed. "What? You out of your mind? You in heaven? You're kidding me, right?"

"Excuse me?"

"Come on, there's no way they could have a heaven without you, boss man."

"I see."

"Not only are you bound for paradise, but you'll have a street named after you. John A. Money Boulevard. Paved in gold and everything. First class all the way, just like you."

"Paved in gold?"

"Darn right. Come on, breathe easy. You are a shoo-in for the golden roads when the Big Guy comes a calling."

"You think so?" asked John. "And you know about the Big Guy? I thought you didn't see him."

"Come again?"

"The big guy, the one in the Hawaiian shirt?"

"The big guy? In a Hawaiian shirt?" asked Howard.

"Yeah, that's the one. The one that takes you to heaven."

"I think you mean the guy in the long black robe who carries a scythe."

"That's what I thought, but…"

"Hey, I saw the movie. The creepy guy, the one in the black moo-moo, swoops you up and you end up in the clouds."

"You mean at the Pearly Gates?"

"Yeah, that, too."

"So you do know? And then what? How do you get in?"

"Get into heaven? Simple as pie. I plan on using your name myself at the gate. Yes, sir, I'll just tell those folks that I personally know Mr. John A. Money, and I'll have no worries in the world. Are you going to heaven…I mean, please? You can bank on that. Know what I mean?"

"Simple as pie?"

"Shoo-in," said Howard.

John opened the door to his office to go back inside. "Thank you, Howard. I think."

"No thanks needed, boss man. Just speaking the truth." Howard smiled broadly and sensed that he was scoring big points. "Wait, I just had a brilliant thought."

"What now?" asked John.

"Okay, this is great. Here's a question: what would heaven be without you?" asked Howard.

John shrugged.

"Hell." Howard beamed. "That's right. Without you, heaven would be...hell."

"Thank you again, Howard." John walked into his office.

Howard followed, pulling out his keys and jingling them. "I uh, heard what you did for Jenkins. '95 Toyota Corolla."

"Excuse me?" John asked.

"I drive a '95 Toyota Corolla. It has 143,000 miles on it." He tossed the keys toward John, but John stepped aside, and they landed with a jangle on the floor and slid under his credenza.

John shook his head and left the office. Howard followed, leaving his keys on the floor.

John walked up to the receptionist's desk "Marge, clear my calendar." He headed toward the elevators but stopped and turned back to Marge.

"Who was it that came in a couple of weeks ago looking for a donation? Some kind of homes for the poor?"

"Habitat?" asked Marge.

"Yeah, have Accounting cut them a check for five hundred dollars."

"Excuse me? Five hundred?"

Howard stepped up to John. "Sir, do you need a ride? I have a Toyota Corolla. 1995. With 143,000 miles."

Marge stood up. "Sir, what do I do about Dixon?"

John looked at her. "And give a hundred dollars to that Global Warming thing...and to the Boy Scouts and...oh yeah, the Girl Scouts." He turned back toward the elevator and mumbled to himself, "I wonder if that's enough?"

Marge stepped out from behind her desk. "What about Dixon?"

John pushed the button on the elevator. It opened and he stepped in.

Howard bolted back toward the office to get his keys. "Wait, Mr. Money. I can give you a ride"

As the elevator doors closed, Marge scratched her head with her pencil. "How do I get on this gravy train?"

Chapter 10

John punched the lobby button in the elevator and considered his options. He had one day. Twenty-four hours. According to the consensus of his band of flunkies, good people get into heaven. How good did he have to be, he wondered? Not a murderer? Not a bigamist? Not an arsonist? He wasn't any of those things. Of course, he could list a few things he'd done in his lifetime that he didn't want to think of at the moment. He wondered if bad things lots of years ago could be made up by recent good things. How was good measured against bad? It seemed like a hard equation.

Up to this point, John A. Money had given little thought to his final destination. He hadn't even taken out preneed funeral insurance. He was too young for such a thing. Not only had he not made plans for how he'd be buried in the ground, he'd given little thought to what happened after that. Maybe he should have paid more attention to what the preacher said every Sunday rather than use the sermon time to plan advertising campaigns for his clients. Somewhere in his mind, he remembered hearing heaven preached about in church, but it always seemed to be something old wrinkled people would be interested in. Not him. He always figured that when he was in his eighties, sitting in a rocking chair on the porch, he'd have time to plan for heaven.

John glanced at his watch. The face bore the image of a fifty-dollar gold piece. He bought it to remind himself of his great success in accumulating a small fortune over the past forty-seven years of his life. Making money was like a game of Monopoly, and he owned Park Place and Boardwalk. How could it get any better, except for collecting more rent from all the suckers that landed on his property? And he did it for his family. He was successful for them. He'd worked his way up to a giant house in a prestigious neighborhood. He could afford to send his daughters to any college. His wife didn't have to work. She could play at the hairdresser or bridge club or wherever she wanted. He'd given them the good life. That should count for something, he thought. Sure, he'd had to sacrifice. He didn't spend much time with them anymore. When was that last family trip? Two years? Five years ago? Vanessa had been after him to set aside some time for a family vacation. Now, there wasn't much point thinking about it.

John gritted his teeth. He'd never surrendered to circumstances before, and he wasn't about to waste his last few hours. If good deeds were needed, he could stock up on them. One thing he'd learned from making deals is that you can never have too much ammunition on your side. He had twenty-four hours to do as many good deeds as possible. After he'd stocked up on good deeds, there were a few family matters he wanted to clear up before saying good-bye to his family.

The elevator door opened, and John walked out looking for opportunities. As he hurried through the building lobby, he almost tripped over a small girl. She dropped a box, and John bent down to help her pick up small packages of candy that spread all over the floor. Another girl and a man that had to be their dad helped with the pickup.

"I'm so sorry," said John.

"That's okay, mister" said one of the girls. "Do you want to buy some of our candy? It's to raise money for our baseball team."

John put three packages back into her box and turned toward the door. "Sorry, no time right now— Wait..."that could be a good deed. "What team?"

The other girl spoke up. "The Panthers."

A memory popped into John's mind. "Not the Pretty Panthers of Plano? 'Go

Cats, Go?'"

"That's us. H ow'd you know?"

"My daughters played with the Panthers when they were younger. I used to go to every game. That was…a number of years ago." John looked at the father and pointed to the two girls. "Mister, do you know what you have here?"

The father shrugged, "Three unsold boxes of candy?"

"They grow up so quickly… Enjoy every minute of it. Life is too short."

One of the girls held a box up toward John. "So you'll buy some candy?"

John looked in the box and picked out one of the packages. He reached in his pocket and pulled out a money clip from which he extracted a twenty-dollar bill. "Sure. Is this good enough?"

The girl reached in her own pocket. "I'll get your change."

"Keep it." He walked off with the candy.

"Thanks, mister," said one of the girls.

John thought that the deed felt kind of good. He wondered if that would get him points for heaven. He stopped for a moment, looking for some other opportunity. At the glass doors leading into the lobby he saw a woman carrying several shopping bags trying to open the door, so he rushed over to help. .As she stepped in, one of her bags fell to the floor.

John picked it up and handed it back to her, noticing that there was some kind of pink blanket in one of the bags. He also saw that she had a little bit of a belly.

"My pleasure ma'am. Glad to help. And when are you expecting the little one?"

The lady shifted the bags in her arms. "Excuse me? The what?"

"Your baby, when is it due."

With a suddenness that startled John, the lady stood erect and huffed aloud. Her face turned an angry red as she turned and walked quickly away. "I'm not pregnant!" she said.

John looked around the lobby to see if anyone else saw that he'd just made a jackass of himself. *Well, I guess that good deed doesn't count, but there's got to be more good deeds out there somewhere..*

As soon as he left his building, he saw a couple standing near the steps in an embrace. He couldn't think of anything to do for them. An elderly lady was walking a cocker spaniel, and he thought he might wait until she got to the end of the block and help her across, but dismissed that idea as well. He headed toward the parking garage.

Sitting on a bench at the bus stop, a man in his early thirties wearing a T-shirt and a floppy hat flicked a cigarette butt into the street.

John brushed off the empty side of the bench and sat next to him and smelled the stale aroma of cheap wine. He reached into his pocket, and hiding the wad so no one could see it, he peeled off a hundred-dollar bill. "Excuse me, sir."

The man turned his bloodshot eyes toward John. "Yeah, what?"

"You look like a man who could use a leg up. Now, I'm sure you have some little savings account somewhere for you and the missus, but you need more than that to plan for the future."

The man belched alcohol.

John grimaced at the smell but continued. "Here's what you do." John held up the C-note. "If you'll put this seed money into a CD or stock, and add to it every month—it's called dollar cost averaging—in no time at all the magic of compounded interest and stock growth will create a comfortable nest egg to retire on."

Licking his lips, the man reached for the money, but John held it back.

"Can I count on you to do that? Invest? Save? Plan for retirement? It's the good and proper thing to do."

The man smiled, revealing at least two missing teeth. "Sure, mister..." He grabbed the bill, crumpled it in his hand, and stuffed it in his shirt pocket. "God bless you."

John got up. "Good. Good. That's very good. Remember, invest, dollar cost averaging, the miracle of compound interest."

John knew he was on a roll. No one could accuse him of not only being a good man, but being a nice man as well. As he turned to enter the parking lot, he ran smack-dab into a man carrying a tall stack of CDs and a lugging a laptop under his arm. The whole stack tumbled to the ground, landing next to some broken window glass. The man almost took off running, but John said, "Let me help you pick this stuff up."

The man looked around like he was scared but allowed John to stack the CDs back into his hands and adjust the laptop under his arm.

As John arranged the CDs in the man's arms, he talked to him. "Ever heard of the Good Samaritan? He was in the Bible. He was a good man. Did you know that good men go to heaven?"

As soon as the CDs were picked up, the man bolted out of sight.

John called to him, "You're welcome. Happy to oblige. I'm a good-deed doer, you know." He continued into the parking lot and thought to himself, *Now for the deed I should have done a long time ago.*

Chapter 11

John located Ricky's VW parked in the lot next to the office building. He gazed at the vehicle for a moment and thought back to earlier, simpler times in his life. He remembered how in the 1970s and '80s, Volkswagen Beetles and buses were the rave of young, struggling families. He'd owned several in those first few years out of college. Now they were icons of a past era. A few young friends with families like Ricky still nursed along the old VW buses in their various styles and nicknames: the VW Type 2, the split-window bus, splittie, split, microbus, micro, transporter, bulli, samba, breadloaf, vanagon and transporter. These were an alternative to family minivans and SUVs. John put his hand on the door handle of Rickey's VW bus. The door opened with a metallic creak. (The lock had been sprung years ago.) The box with an engine in the back had seen better days. The once-sky-blue exterior was now covered with worn gray spots, and the once-white roof was riddled with rust.

John wondered how it looked for one of his employees to drive such a dump, much less how it was going to look with him driving it. Nevertheless, a good deed was a good deed, so he climbed up into the black plastic driver's seat and surveyed the instruments. Unlike his Mercedes, he found no GPS, no CD player, no trip odometer, no air conditioning, and no automatic transmission—only a speedometer and a gas gauge. He looked around for the ignition and found it on the top right side of the steering column. It took a while to get the key into the hole, and when he did get it in, it wouldn't turn. He twisted it to the right and to the left. Nothing. He pushed the brake pedal, pushed the clutch pedal. Nothing.

He twisted the steering wheel, and finally the key turned, sending the bus lunging forward. He tried again, this time holding down the clutch. To his surprise, the motor started and hummed along with that characteristic VW chug-a-chug.

His next challenge involved dealing with the stick shift that rose out of the floorboard. He vaguely remembered the shift pattern and studied the worn diagram on the black shift knob. After three tries, he remembered how to push down on the knob and pull back to get it into the reverse gear. He let out on the clutch, and the bus inched backward. Shifting into first gear, he pulled out of the lot. Someone called his name. There on the steps of the office building stood Howard, waving his keys in his hand. John ignored him, pulled onto the street, shifted into second and then third gear, and left Howard running after him in the street.

The pitiful four cylinders could hardly make freeway speed, but John stayed in the right lane, and after an exhausting twenty minutes in the rattletrap, he drove onto the campus where Kelly attended college. . . The bus stopped with a jerk as he let off on the clutch. It took three tries to open the door, and it wasn't until he pushed hard with his shoulder that he got it to budge. Since he'd only been on campus once or twice, he wasn't sure where to go, but he saw a number of students entering a building that looked like a cafeteria.

In the building, he found a food court half-full of students. A crowd milled around the foyer where a large banner proclaiming Community Involvement Month was hanging from the ceiling. About a dozen booths decorated with smaller banners lined the wall. The sign on the first booth read Alpha/Omega Mission Trip. One of the students at the booth caught John's eye as he walked in the door. "Hey, mister, got a minute?"

John looked around the cafeteria for Kelly. "Not really." He turned and read the sign. "Wait...what's this for?"

"The campus ministry group is sponsoring a trip to the coast to repair houses hit by the hurricane."

"Hmm. I already gave to that...I think. Is this a God thing?"

"It's our spring break service project."

"And if I give, I'll get points to go to heaven?" Not waiting for an answer, he pulled out his checkbook and started writing.

"Uh...it couldn't hurt."

A second student stepped over. "I don't think that's how it works, sir."

"You take checks? How about a hundred dollars?"

The first student held out his hand. "Sure...we'll take a check."

The second student looked at the check. "We appreciate this, sir, and giving is good, but to get to heaven I think it takes..."

John stepped away, not listening. At the next booth, two women in nurse uniforms stood looking for a victim. One of the nurses looked like a student. The other was as old as the hills and reminded him of the battleaxe named Nurse Ratched from some book he'd read in college.

The student nurse spoke first, "Take your blood pressure, sir? Live healthy, live long, that's our motto at Tyler Street Health Services..."

John almost laughed. "Live long? You're too late..."

Nurse Ratched spoke with a sadistic smile on her face. "Had a prostate exam? You look the age..."

John grimaced. "There are some things I won't miss."

The older nurse popped a latex glove on her hand. "You're in luck, it's Turn Your Head and Cough Month. Step behind the partition. We're running a special."

John stepped away briskly. "Thanks, I'll keep my head where it is for now."

The sign on the next booth read Wycliffe Bible Translators— Does God Speak Your Language?" John shook his head. "Bible translation? Not that again. Aren't there enough Bibles?"

The man at the booth heard him and stepped out from behind the table. "Sir, you know there are over six thousands people groups in the world who don't have the Bible in their own language."

John stopped and turned. "Six thousand? Like whom? The Tatar people of Idaho?"

"Funny you should mention the Tatar group. One of our students asked about them last week. The Tatar people actually live in Asia. They're descendants of Genghis Khan. If anyone needs the Bible…"

"Descendants of Genghis Khan? And you're raising money to do this translation?"

"We support people called by God to translate the Bible."

"Called by God, huh? And you need money to help with this?"

"We need money, people, and prayers."

John pulled out his checkbook and started writing. "Okay, I've got to earn as many Bible brownie points as I can today. This should be worth double points." He peeled off a sizeable check and handed it to the translator.

"Sir, we appreciate that, but we're really not about getting brownie points. God wants you, not your money."

"Yeah…tell it to someone else. I've already got marching orders." He continued into the cafeteria, still looking for Kelly.

As he looked into the crowd, a lady who'd read too many books on how to be a successful salesperson took a step in front of John and blocked his path. "Sir, sir, step over here. You look like a man with a lot on your mind. What you need, we have right here. It's a timeshare."

John tried to sidestep the saleslady, "Not interested. I'm looking for…"

She persisted. "That's right—a timeshare for the time of your life. Take the kids to the beach, to the mountains; we've got timeshares all over the world."

"I'm going to die tomorrow," John stated matter-of-factly.

The saleslady didn't miss a beat. "We're all going to die tomorrow, sir. Take a little time for yourself, enjoy life. Life is too short not to enjoy it."

John stared at her. "Dead. As in doornail."

"Go to Florida, go to California, go to Poughkeepsie, Walla-Walla, Washington, or to the shores of Borneo. We've got timeshares all over the world."

"Listen, lady, I know a guy named Lucky I'd like you to meet."

The saleswoman showed interest. "Lucky? You know a guy named Lucky? Do you think he wants a timeshare, 'cause we've got timeshares. Anyplace he wants to go, we got it. Married, divorced? Good credit, bad credit. Doesn't matter. We can get him in."

John managed to step away. "It would be a good deed for me to have Lucky pay you a visit…"

She called to John as he walked on, "Good deed it is, then, send Lucky to me. We'll put him in a timeshare. Yessir, we can do it if anybody can…yessiree. Bob."

John heard a voice. "Mr. Money?"

He turned to see a young man seated at a table. He looked vaguely familiar. "Have we met?"

"Yes, sir. I was at your house for Kelly's July fourth cookout."

"Wait a minute, you're Denver."

"Excuse me?"

"Your name is Denver."

"No, sir, the name's Austin."

"Exactly."

Austin was confused. "Sir, what are you doing here?"

"This is where my daughter goes to school, right? So, any idea where I might find her?"

Austin pointed to another building outside the cafeteria. "Yeah, the girls' dorm, room 212."

John turned to exit. "Thanks."

"Sir, there are no men allowed in there right now."

John turned to Austin. "I'm not a man. I'm a father." As he walked off, he thought to himself, *at least I used to be.*

John parked in a no parking zone…

Chapter 12

John entered the girls' dorm as a man on a mission. He stepped into the lobby and headed straight for the main staircase. His presence immediately stirred the ire of the redheaded receptionist sitting behind the counter. She didn't cotton to anything happening in her dorm that smacked of rule breaking, and a man in the dorm broke her favorite rule. She jumped up from her Sudoku puzzle and shouted to John, "Sir, you can't go up there! This is a girls-only dorm. And this isn't the mixed visitation hours."

John barely acknowledged her. He kept walking.

She fiddled with the door to get out from behind the counter. "But, sir...there are no men...stop now, mister...or, or...I'm calling security."

John turned toward her. "Listen, I paid for half of this building, and I've got something to say to my daughter. I'm going up."

The receptionist's face turned the color of her hair, "Oh, no you're not. There are to be no men allowed in this dorm at this time."

"I'm not a man. I'm a dad."

She turned back to the counter, picked up the phone, and dialed campus security. John headed up the stairs.

On the second floor, he found room 212 and knocked. He straightened his tie, took a deep breath, and prepared to knock again. The powerful hand of a large man grabbed his wrist and stopped him in mid knock. John spun around and looked up into the face of a campus security guard.

"Sir, you need to come with me."

"Wait a minute. What's going on here? I'm not going anywhere. I came here to talk to my daughter."

Several doors opened on the hall, and girls in various stages of dress stared out of their rooms to see what was happening.

John struggled to get away from the security guard's grip, but the guard swung John's hand around his back and grabbed the other arm, holding them both behind his back as he deftly clicked the handcuffs closed. "Sir, we need to go back to the lobby and work this out."

"Not until I talk with my daughter." He knocked on the door with his head. And the guard jerked him away from it.

The door opened, and Kelly looked out. "Dad?"

"Do you know this man?"

Kelly looked at her dad in the handcuffs and didn't know whether to laugh or cry. "I did."

John's eyes pleaded with his daughter "Kelly?"

She stepped out of the door. "He's my dad."

"Your dad?"

Kelly nodded. The security guard unlocked the cuffs, but kept hold of his right arm. "Nevertheless, sir, you cannot be in this hall."

"This is a girls' dorm, Dad. Not coed. There are only certain visiting hours."

"Yeah, yeah. I get it." With his free arm, he reached into his pants pocket and pulled out a fifty-dollar bill. He stretched it toward the guard.

"Could this make it a co-dad dorm for an hour?"

The guard gave John a sneer and looked to Kelly. "You can take this to the common area. That's the best that I can do. Do you understand?"

John extended the fifty dollars again. The guard took a step back and pointed down the hall. Kelly headed in that direction and John followed. The guard followed them until they arrived at a common area that consisted of several couches and tables. Kelly collapsed on the sofa and looked up at her father. "Dad, what are you doing here?"

John stood. "I wanted to talk."

"You mean command? Or bribe me like you tried with the guard? Not everyone thinks as much of the almighty dollar. Besides, I tried the talking part this morning. You didn't seem to want to hear what I had to say."

John paced. "Touché, I deserved that. You're not a big fan of mine right now, are you?"

"Dad, why are you here?"

"Remembering."

Kelly looked confused. "Remembering?"

"I've been thinking about this for the past twenty minutes. I want to tell you a story. I've got to tell you a story."

"Dad, I have a class in thirty minutes. I don't have time for one of your stories."

John turned toward her. "I'll make you a deal. This will be the last story I will ever tell you."

Kelly rolled her eyes "As if..."

"Cross my heart."

"Hope to die?"

John paused, and the blood rushed to his face. "Not really."

Kelly sensed something about her father.. Maybe it was his eyes. Something. Something she hadn't seen in him for—it might have been ten years. She leaned a little forward toward him.

John sat on the couch next to her. "This story begins fifteen years ago…when we lived in that old frame house over on Maple. Remember?"

"Green trim, lots of trees in the backyard? Yeah."

John smiled. "I didn't…remember…until about an hour ago. It all came flooding back. I remember coming home after a long, hard day and no sooner had my key hit the lock, I was greeted by a running little girl screaming…Daddddddyyyyy! She jumped in my arms, covered me with kisses, and no matter what the day had been…my world was right. You remember that?

"Vaguely. I was what—five at the time?"

"I remember it well. Now fast forward...second grade, Mrs...what was her name?"

"Tuppie, Mrs. Tuppie. I remember because all the kids called her guppy."

"Open house...on your desk was a story. Remember?"

Kelly nodded, "I remember the title—"My Hero"

John completed the name of the title. "My Dad"

Kelly almost smiled.

"Kelly, you know I've made my living writing marketing plans and guiding major accounts. But never before nor since has four words had such an impact. 'My hero...'"

Kelly completed it this time. "'...My Dad.' But why now, Dad? What's gotten into you since this morning? And why now? I've got class..."

"Hang on. This is my last story, so let me tell it. Now, fast forward five years, grade seven. Your first date..."

Kelly plopped back into the couch, remembering, "Oh my gosh, William Freely? The Junior High Valentine's Dance?"

John laughed. "I remember thinking that he was a zit with legs."

"Be nice. He was only thirteen. I was no prize either."

"Oh, please, you were a treasure. And do you remember our talk after the date?"

Kelly's brow wrinkled. "Not much. I remember the Freelys dropped me off at the door."

"Ten p.m., right on time. You came in, and I was 'waiting up' and asked, so how was your first kiss?"

Kelly remembered. "Oh, that."

"You said?"

"I said 'I wouldn't know.'"

"And I said, 'no kiss?' And you said 'Nope, not gonna waste it on the wrong one.'"

Kelly nodded.

"And I said 'How do you know he is the wrong one?'"

"Cause he's not like you."

A tear formed in John's eyes. "I said, 'like me? Why me?'"

A lump rose in Kelly's throat. "I said, 'Because you love me 'cause I'm me.'"

"And I did love you, Kelly, and I do. I still love you. But somewhere between that seventh grade year and this morning, I found the world's version of success. We moved out of the little wood-frame house on Maple and into our first big brick dream house. I made a name for myself, spent late nights and weekends growing my company, earned lots of money, and put you and your sister in the finest schools. I gave you everything you wanted that money could buy. But on the drive over here, I realized that I'd also taken away the only thing you needed and I needed... Time. My ambition stole precious time away from you, and from everyone in our family. And so my story has a reason. I just want you to know that I've realized my mistake, and that I never stopped loving you."

Kelly had never before seen a tear fall from her father's face. As he spoke to her, a steady stream of them flowed from his eyes, and he kept pushing them away with his hand. "Somehow I had forgotten that little girl who thought I could do it all. Today I remembered all the great times we had when you were in grade school: the sports, the piano recitals, and all the rest. I remember that little girl who played her heart out as a shortstop for the Pretty Panthers of Plano."

Instinctively they said together, "Go, Cats, Go!" They laughed.

"And then I remembered all the things I missed once success took over my life."

Kelly dropped her gaze to the floor. "Dad..."

John continued, "I know I need to wrap this up before the rent-a-cop comes back and drags me off in chains." He forced a chuckle. "Kelly, the reason I came by was to apologize for my actions and words this morning. I want you to know that you're still, and will always be, my baby...and I know that I can't mold my desires into your life. Now, I'll be honest, Bible translation was not on my radar for your life. I'm trying to understand that—but you have to follow your own path and do what you have to do.

Kelly corrected him, "Called to do."

"Okay...not sure what that is. But, if you translate, be the best translator there is."

Kelly leaned over on the couch, put her arms around John, and kissed one of the tears on his cheek. "Thanks, Dad."

"And you and Denver come by for dinner tonight, and we'll talk more."

"Austin, Dad. His name is Austin."

John smiled. "Whatever, just be there tonight. It's got to be tonight."

John put his arm around Kelly's waist. "I love you, baby."

"I love you, too, Daddy."

After a moment, they both stood. Their cheeks were damp with tears, and they wiped them with their hands. Kelly turned to go back to her room to get her books. "Daddy? You're still my hero."

John's face turned bright "No, baby, you're mine."

Kelly blew him a kiss as she walked down the hall. "You are so amazing."

"I realized that I'd also taken away the only thing you needed and I needed... time."

Chapter 13

The rattletrap VW Type 2 Bus clunked into the posh Money neighborhood with John fighting the steering wheel and clutch all the way. He managed to park in the street at the front of his house, afraid that if he put it in the driveway, he'd never get it into reverse again. He banged open the door and almost fell out of the driver's seat into the grass. He slammed the door shut, and it popped back open. The second try did the trick. After he climbed the stairs up to his front door, he stood on the porch for a minute looking out into the street at his German "people's" car.

Martha heard the commotion outside and walked out onto the porch behind John. She glanced around him at what he was looking at. "What in the world is that?"

John didn't take his gaze off the *blunderwagen*. "That, Martha, is technically a 1979 Volkswagen Type 2b Microbus. Some call it a classic."

Martha thought it was the ugliest vehicle she'd ever seen on the road outside her last trip to the backwaters of Costa Rica. "Should I have it towed?"

John chuckled. "No, it's mine. I sorta traded with a friend."

"At gunpoint?"

"No. Is Vanessa home?"

"I think I heard her pull into the garage a minute ago."

John turned to go into the house. "Martha, could you give Charlie a call and set up an appointment to have the car serviced and washed, please? Any time after tomorrow."

"Yes, sir." After John walked into the house, Martha leaned over the balcony to get a better look at the strange vehicle. "Wouldn't you just rather have it burned?"

John entered the living room; walked up to a bookcase, and starting from the top down, read the spines of all the books. After a minute of not finding what he wanted, he picked up a family photo from a table next to the bookshelf. As he looked at the picture, remembering the Christmas dinner and the cold day that they all stood on the front balcony to have the photo taken, the grandfather clock chimed the quarter hour. He looked at it and thought about how he would miss the little things of life, things he had barely noticed before.

From the other end of the house, he could hear Vanessa enter through the kitchen and walk toward him. She was talking on her cell phone.

"Oh, honey, let me tell you...I was simply mortified..." She spotted John. "Penny, let me call you back. John's home. Bye."

She flipped her phone shut and put it in her purse as she placed the bag on a chair. "You're home early."

John shrugged. "Crazy day."

"Oh, please...we could swap tales on crazy days. Remember the hair appointment I told you about?"

John stepped to a smaller bookshelf and kept looking.

Vanessa continued, "Well, I show up, and Jennifer is out sick. Who knows what she has... So, Joanne says she would cut it... Come on, Joanne cut my hair? Please. The last time I let her near my hair, I wore a hat for three weeks. So I said listen... John, are you listening to me?"

He continued looking at the bookshelf. "No. Do we have a Bible?

Vanessa did a double take. "A what? Of course...somewhere. Anyhow, next, I take Mitzy to be groomed at the Paw and Poodle thinking at least one of us ought to get our hair done. But they had no openings until five. So I ask if they can keep her overnight. They say yes...but they need her shot records. So I fly home for the records, and then I remember I'm supposed to drop Mandy off at dance, which I do only to find out class is canceled because Mrs. Peabody's sister is having bariatric surgery. Bless her heart, she's been needing that for years. So I leave Mandy at Morgan's to study. Which brings me back home to find a speaker for the PTA meeting tonight. Is that a crazy enough day for you? I bet you can't beat that."

John looked up at Vanessa. "Where's Mandy? She's got a Bible."

"I told you...she's at Morgan's."

"Oh." He looked at her with serious eyes. "You ever think about dying?"

"Excuse me?"

"You know, death. You ever think about it?"

"Umm...no. Not lately."

"What about heaven? I mean we believe in heaven, right?"

"Okay, John...what are you doing?"

"I mean, we must. We believe in God...right? Humor me."

"Of course we do. We're not heathens."

"That's right. And we go to church...that's a God deal. And we give to charities...that's a

God thing. And heaven is a God place. So, it would make sense that we would believe in heaven."

"Okay. So?"

"Since we've been good...at least I've been good lately...we should go to heaven...when we die. Right?"

"One would hope."

"Hope? That's all you got? Some things you need to know."

"John, you're scaring me here. What's this all about?"

John faked a laugh. "Oh, nothing important. Just an academic question. But...we do believe, right?"

"Yes, John, we believe in heaven if it will make you happy."

John looked at Vanessa's hair. "I thought you went to get your hair cut today."

"What? I just told you..."

John headed for the back door.

"Now where are you going?"

"I need a little air." He opened the door, paused, walked back to her, and put his arms around her. "Vanessa? You know I love you, right?"

She returned the hug. "And I love you." They stayed still for a few moments, then John let go and stepped back toward the door. "John, are you sure you're okay?"

"Yeah, just got some things on my mind to work through." He walked out the door, and it closed. A few seconds later, John opened it again and stuck in his head. "Where's Mitzy?"

Chapter 14

John wandered around his back yard looking at things he didn't even know he owned. He noticed a nice chrome barbeque grill out by the pool he'd never used. He remembered the old green grill they got when they were first married. He'd cooked many a hamburger on that one. For Fourth of July parties, birthday parties, Memorial Day family get-togethers, and occasionally Friday nights just for the heck of it. He studied the shiny new grill. He had some vague recollection of Vanessa having it delivered for some swimming party for the college kids from the church. He did remember that she even hired some "hamburger man" to cook on it because John had to go on a trip to Houston. A little farther back in the yard, near a retaining wall, he found several pots of blooming flowers that he thought might be begonias. He and Vanessa used to plant flowers together every year. Now someone else did it, and he paid them.

Next to a concrete bench, he discovered a small pond. He sat down on the bench and watched the bubbling fountain for a minute. The surface of the pond was half-covered with lily pads, and under the pads, he saw several gold-and-white fish. They swam back and forth as he counted them. He heard the latch lifted on the gate and looked up to see Mandy and her friend Morgan come into the backyard.

At first the two girls didn't see John, but just before they went into the back door, Mandy saw him and turned back. "Hey, Pop, what's up?"

"Oh, hi, sweetie, how was dance class?"

"It was canceled. I've been at Morgan's working on our biology project."

Morgan waved. "Hi, Mr. Money. What are you doing out here all by yourself?"

They walked over to him, and Mandy sat down beside him on the bench. "Yeah, Dad, you're never home this early, and I've never seen you on this bench."

John shrugged. "Just having a little me time. Doing some thinking. You know?"

"About?" asked Mandy.

John shrugged again. "Just stuff." He pointed into the pond. "Did you know there are seven goldfish in there?"

"Uhh...yeah! I think they're called Koi. Remember? Kelly built that pond as a summer project, like five years ago? She named them after the seven dwarfs?"

"Right. Seven dwarfs. I remember something about that."

"So, what are you doing out here, Dad?" asked Mandy.

John didn't seem to hear the question. "Mandy, you know I love you, right?"

"Sure, and I love you, too. Dad...you all right?"

He took a breath and forced himself not to reach out and hug Mandy. He didn't want her to know that this was her dad's last day. At least, not yet. He turned on his salesman's charm and snapped back to his old self. "Absolutely...top of the world. And...what about you?"

"I'm good," said Mandy.

"By the way, Mandy, I, uh, wanted to ask you something. Do you, you know, believe in heaven?"

"Heaven? Uh, yeah...sure."

"How do you know?"

"Well, Dad, I think believing in heaven comes from knowing God. He loves you, and you love Him back, and you believe in His heaven."

"Just like that? Then it's something that feels right?"

Mandy smiled. "No, Dad. Not quite. Feelings can be wrong. This is something you know deep down. It's called faith."

"Okay. So if there's a heaven made by God, who is a good guy, you gotta believe it is full of good people. Since only good people would believe in the good guy, right?"

Mandy thought for a second. "Sure. I suppose."

John continued, "And I've been a pretty good Dad to you and Kelly?"

Mandy nodded.

"So, it would make sense...that I will end up there... When I die, I mean."

"I guess."

John looked frustrated. "You guess? All you have is a guess? How about a yes? I would love to hear a yes."

Morgan spoke up. "Excuse me, Mr. Money, but Mrs. Tomlinson says that just being good won't get you into heaven."

"Morgan's right, Dad. Mrs. Tomlinson says you must accept Christ as savior to be guaranteed salvation."

"That's what you want, salvation," said Morgan. "Heaven is just a bonus."

John sighed. "Pretty good bonus, I'd say."

Morgan continued, "Mrs. Tomlinson says it's all about grace. We accept Christ, and the Father's grace brings us into the family."

"Oh, grace...that's no problem. We say grace at Sunday dinner, usually."

Mandy wrinkled her brow. "Dad..."

"Okay, kidding, just kidding. But, let's hit the high points. My parents, their parents, and probably every Money ever born went to the same church. So, I'd say this Christian thing is a shoo-in."

Mandy shook her head. "I'm pretty sure it runs a little deeper than that, Pop."

Morgan added, "Yeah, Mr. Money, Mrs. Tomlinson says we can't get by on the good name of our ancestors. She says it's the one walk we walk alone."

The wheels were turning in John's head as Mandy spoke. "Right, Dad, she says only those who have personally asked Jesus into their hearts will have life abundant and everlasting."

"You say we have to ask Jesus? Into our hearts? I've heard something about that before. So...who is this Mrs. Tomlinson?"

"Our Sunday School teacher," answered Morgan.

"Well...I guess she would know then, huh?"

Mandy opened her backpack. "She would...but, as she always tells us...go to the source..." Mandy pulled out a Bible.

John's eyes lit up. "A Bible! I knew we had one of those."

Morgan sat down on the retaining wall by the pond. "Mr. Money, it's not about *who* you are; it's about *whose* you are."

John didn't get it.

Mandy put the Bible on her Dad's knees and pointed at some of the writing on the open page. "Look, see what it says here in the Bible? I circled it. 'If you confess with your mouth, Jesus is Lord, and believe in your heart that God raised him from the dead, you will be saved.' How simple is that?"

John nodded, but was still unsure. "Seems like a... piece of cake." What he really thought was *this is harder than it sounds.*

"Dad, money, power, and being good are all fine, but heaven is for those who love God. Get it?"

"Got it," John answered instinctively.

"Good. Then He's in your heart?"

"Sure."

Mandy smiled. "Then, you will be a resident of heaven when you die...many years from now."

"You betcha," agreed John in words. He always did have the knack of answering what the customer wanted to hear, whether he believed it or not.

Mandy stood and hugged her dad. "Well, we need to get to work on our project. Come on, Morgan." Mandy grabbed her backpack and they walked toward the house.

Mandy turned and looked at John. "You coming in, Dad?"

"No, not yet. I've got some business to take care of... Mandy? I love you."

Mandy smiled as she opened the back door. "Love you more, Dad. See ya later..."

After Mandy and Morgan were gone, John noticed Mandy's Bible on the bench. He picked it up and stood to take it to Mandy. Instead he sat back down and opened it up. He turned through the pages. He'd heard all the stories from the Bible his whole life. Noah. David, Mary, and Joseph. But he only thought of the Bible as a history book. Maybe it was like Marge said, something that people sold just to make money. Then again, Mandy went right to it for answers. He flipped through its pages and wondered, *Was the Bible really full of answers?*

John Money did something he hardly ever remembered doing before. Except for repeating written words in church or saying a memorized prayer at the dinner table, he hadn't talked to God very many times. He didn't want to call what he said a prayer, but somehow, somewhere, he asked God to help him understand what this day was all about. Why did everyone seem to have answers about the afterlife except the person that was staring it in the face? *This is too much for me to understand*, he thought.

He closed the Bible and looked back into the pond. Seven goldfish. John counted them again. There they were, swimming their lives away, oblivious to death looming in their midst. John imagined that he'd been swimming through life like those fish. He'd never given any thought to death or what happened on the other side of death. He'd been swimming through life as stupid as a goldfish.

He picked up Mandy's Bible and headed for...he wasn't sure where he'd go. There had to be some real answers out there. He never put much stock in Marge's hair-brained cosmic babblings. Howard's opinions were no more than brownnosing. Ricky's was too gullible to believe. Who did that leave to tell him the truth? A teenage daughter? He walked out of the backyard through the side gate and headed toward the rusted blue-and-white VW bus not knowing where it might take him.

"It's called faith, Dad."

Chapter 15

With John grinding through four gears, the rattletrap bus made it on to the freeway, but as hard as John tried, he couldn't make it go over fifty. A guy wearing Ray-Bans and driving a convertible Lexus pulled behind him and honked several times. The car pulled alongside the bus, and another moppy-haired guy in the passenger seat yelled to him, "Get off the road, Grandpa."

John ignored the idiots and didn't give them a glance as they sped away. A mile later, the bus gave up. He heard a ka-thump from the engine compartment in the rear, and the motor puttered to a halt just as he managed to pull it over onto the shoulder of the freeway. He sat for a moment with cars whizzing by, then tried to start the motor again. All he got was a lethargic rumble from the engine as it turned over a few times, then stopped as soon as he let go of the key. *What else is going to die around me today?* He thought.

Not wanting to step into oncoming traffic, John lifted his legs over the gearshift, moved to the passenger seat, and pushed the reluctant door open. He stepped out and had to walk through some kind of flowering purple nettle to get to the back of the van. He lifted the rectangular door to the motor compartment and took a look. The rusty motor box was full of pipes and wires and pulleys. He didn't have a clue what he was looking for. He reached into his pocket for his cell phone, but the battery was dead—or maybe it had never recovered from Lucky's involvement.

Every few seconds another car whizzed by at sixty-five miles an hour. An eight-foot fence bordered the highway, so as far as he could tell, he was stuck like a frog in a cactus. He pulled a handkerchief from his pocket, put it on the asphalt, and knelt down to take a closer look at the engine. Somewhere in his college years, he'd read *Zen and the Art of Volkswagen Maintenance* but it didn't stick. He had no clue what to look for. There was gunky grease caking the bottom of the compartment and black soot covered everything else. He wiggled a wire and tapped on a black plastic hose, not knowing what it might do or how it might help, but it made him feel like he was doing something. At that moment, he heard the thunder rumble of motorcycle engines behind him. He stood up and grabbed his now dirty handkerchief.

He turned and saw two guys straight out of Hell's Angels cocking their kickstands on two black-and-chrome muscle machines. One of the bikers wore a black leather vest, had hair down to his shoulders, and sported a bushy mustache that covered half his face. The other was a rather tall and intimidating black man who was bald as a billiard ball and wore a shirt with its sleeves torn off. John stood and braced himself for a confrontation. He wondered if he'd have better luck running into traffic, but the thought of being hurled a hundred feet in the air by a sixty-mile-per-hour vehicle didn't seem appealing—even if he did have less than a day to live.

The two brutes stepped up to John, glanced at him a half a second, and then bent down to look at the open motor compartment.

The bald one looked up at him. "Bro, where'd you get this cool ride?"

John stammered, "Cool… ride? Yes, well I traded with a friend for it today."

The biker with the mustache looked at John. "Sixteen hundred cc."

"CC?"

"The motor. It's a 1600cc. Air cooled. Sweet. Used to have one until my Susan ran off with that guy from Montana in it back in '87."

"Your Susan?" asked John.

"Just a friend, you understand. But we had a thing going, Susan and me."

"Type 2 or 4?" asked the bald one.

"The bus, Type 2, the motor Type 4; 1.7 liters, 68 horsepower."

"68 horsepower?" said John, "No wonder it wouldn't go over fifty."

"It would," said the mustached one.

"Would what?" asked John.

"Go over fifty—if it was tuned properly. This thing's got some serious work needed."

"You're telling me," said John.

The bald one looked up and down John's thousand-dollar suit. "What're you doing out here in the traffic? It ain't safe...for a guy dressed up spiffy like you are."

"Here? Well, it was the motor...it just stopped. It was running fine, then I heard a ka-thump, then nothing."

"Ka-thump?" asked the mustached biker as he prodded with his finger at various metal and plastic objects in the motor compartment.

"Ka-thump, then nothing," restated John.

"Ka-thump...ka-thump," the mustached one said over and over to himself as he examined the motor. The bald one knelt down, and they were both looking in the compartment saying "ka-thump" to each other and poking at greasy-looking thingamajigs.

The mustached one looked up at John. "Not ka-thump, bang?"

John thought a moment. "No, just ka-thump, then nothing."

The bald one stepped away for a moment and then came back with a set of tools.

"Not ka-thump, bang," said the mustached one to the bald one. "Just ka-thump."

The bald one looked up at John. "Any clangs, any backfires?"

John thought again. "No, just ka-thump."

"Ka-thump," they both said to themselves. This time they were poking around with a screwdriver. John figured that if they meant to kill him and take his American Express card, they would have done it by now.

"1972." Said the mustached one, looking up at John.

John corrected him. "It's a 1979."

"I know that—I'm talking the motor. They came out with the Type 4 in 1972." By now, the mustached mechanic had his entire arm stuck up into the compartment, feeling around for something.

"That so?" asked John, not knowing how else to respond.

"Same motor used in some Porsche 914s," said the bald one.

"Porsche?" John was interested.

"Yeah, he designed Volkswagen, you know—back in the 30s."

"That so?"

"Wait, wait a minute." The mustached one was excited. His entire right arm was stuck into the compartment, and he was feeling around with irrational exuberance, or at least that's how John saw it. "Wait…here it is. Got it." He extracted his arm, which was now covered with grimy soot. "Wire," he announced.

"Why are we what?" asked John.

"Wire….wire…there was a loose wire."

John didn't want to irritate him, so he just nodded.

The mustached one stood up. "That'll do it; I bet a nickel. Try it."

John got back into the van from the passenger side, reached over, and turned the key. The motor revved and started. He crawled out and stepped back to the two bikers. "Hey, thanks for your help. What can I pay you?" John reached into his front pocket, produced his money clip, and peeled off a fifty.

"Pay us? For what?" asked the bald biker.

"Fixing it," said John.

"You kidding? I haven't had this much fun in a month of Sundays. Everyone needs a little help now and then," said the mustached one.

"You don't want anything?" asked John.

"Thanks will do, Bro," said the bald one. He held out a fist.

John tentatively made a fist and touched it to the bald man's hand. "Thanks."

"Need any more help?" asked the mustached biker.

"No, no. Thanks, you've done plenty. I think I know where I'm going," John lied.

"Always the best plan," said the bald one. "As Mrs. Tomlinson used to say, 'Know where you're going, 'cause if you don't, you never know where you'll end up.'"

"Mrs. Tomlinson?"

"My Sunday School teacher when I was in rehab. She helped me turn my life around."

"Wow, that lady gets around."

"Yeah, I'd be headed for hell if it wasn't for her." The bald man pulled a well-worn book out of his back pocket. "Go to the source, she always told us." He opened a frayed New Testament. "I didn't think my life was worth dick until she told me how God loved even messed-up birds like me. You sure you don't need any help getting where you're going?"

"No. Thanks. You've been a lot of help," said John. "I was just lucky you happened along."

"Not lucky," said the mustached biker. "Everything happens for a reason. God works in mysterious ways."

"See ya around," said the bald one. He pointed to his New Testament. "Always go to the source," he said, then put the book back into his pocket.

The two bikers dusted off their hands, got back on the bikes, and pulled out into the traffic.

John returned to the bus and sat in the driver's seat for a moment, watching the cars whiz past him. *Go to the source*, he thought. He eased the bus into traffic, knowing where he'd go next.

John eased out in traffic, knowing where he'd go next…

Chapter 16

The old Volkswagen took forever to get up to fifty miles per hour, and then took an exit before John could even think about it. As if driven by the bus itself, John turned down an old familiar street that he hadn't seen in a decade. It passed by Bryan Elementary School, where John learned how to make a profit selling nickel candy bars for ten cents to his classmates. Around the corner and to the right, it headed down Kellogg Street, where John had grown up.

This old neighborhood was not in the best part of the city anymore. Even so, as John saw the old familiar houses he remembered an earlier, simpler time of life. The freshly painted houses from his childhood now bore the signs of rental houses. Gary Collins, who lived in the house with the gabled roof, was now a county commissioner. Gary's mother had always kept the front yard meticulously decorated in colorful flowers. As John drove past that house, he saw an old blue Ford pickup truck in the driveway, its engine sitting next to it on the pavement. He passed by Allen and Roy's house. Robert's house. Sharon's. Vickie's. Old Mrs. McVeigh's house.

The VW Microbus pulled up to the curb and stopped in front of house number 3337. Like most of the houses on this block, it was a post

World War II cracker box with a one-car detached garage. His mom had told him how they moved into this starter home when his dad came home from the Korean War a decade before John was born. John studied the house carefully. It needed painting. The fig tree that his mother loved so much and that grew to the left of the front porch was long gone. Instead of the screen door on the front porch that he remembered slamming a million times, the front door was protected by a black wrought-iron cage. The windows were also barred, and the yard was mostly dirt with patches of weeds. How many times did he and his friends lay on that thick carpet of Bermuda grass watching the twinkling stars?

John tried to remember the last time he'd driven by the house. It was after his mother's funeral, eighteen years ago. She was dead. His father was dead. He'd soon be joining them. He hoped. He wondered if he'd see his mother and father again in the great beyond. He wondered if there was a great beyond.

Even at his parents' funerals, John hadn't considered death for himself. It seemed too final. Too far in the future. He had a realization that even this old rattletrap VW bus was going to outlive him. As he looked at his old house, he remembered it as a place of life. There on the front porch, dressed in a new Easter suit bought from old Mr. Lewis at Montgomery Ward, he'd smiled like a cat that had just caught a canary at his mother holding an old Kodak box camera. He still had that picture. Somewhere.

John came out of his daydream when he heard someone walking beside the van. He turned to look and found himself staring down the barrel of a revolver. Two young teenage boys with angry faces stared back at him.

"Your wallet," one of them yelled.

John froze, not knowing how to react.

"Now, or I shoot," said the one holding the gun.

John reached into his back pocket and took out his wallet. He held it up, and one of them grabbed it from him.

The boy opened it and pulled out a wad of cash, then one by one, he pulled out an ATM card and several credit cards.

"What else you got? Just this stinking car?"

John held up his hands. "Take whatever you want." He wondered if they would really shoot him. Although he still didn't quite understand the Angel of Death thing, surely Lucky wouldn't let someone else kill him before his allotted time. He reconsidered. *Suppose I get shot and linger in an emergency room and keel over at precisely 9:48 a.m.?* He didn't have any desire to experience a bullet hole in any part of his body. "Take whatever you want," he said again.

"What's the PIN number on the ATM card?" asked the one with the gun, holding up one of John's cards. "Tell me or I shoot."

"It's…it's…3337." It dawned on John how ironic it was. He'd remembered that house number all these years, using it as his secret PIN number. Now, sitting in front of that old house, he was about to experience the last vestiges of life. *That must be how it ends. He didn't have heart trouble. It would have to be some kind of accident. How else would he suddenly die?* He closed his eyes, waiting for the inevitable bullet.

In his final remaining seconds, John prayed. He prayed that during his last few hours of life that God would keep him conscious enough to say good-bye to his family. He prayed for help. He didn't know what kind of help or what form of help. That movie about his life he thought Lucky should provide actually did flash through his mind. He remembered the old house as it used to be. He saw his parents driving out of the driveway on a Sunday morning. He was dressed in his Montgomery Ward suit and one of his daddy's red-and-white striped ties. He saw himself sitting in a pew next to his mother and father. He remembered coloring in a coloring book during the sermon. He remembered looking up and could have sworn that the old preacher was pointing at him. He remembered the preacher's words, "Whenever you need help, son, go to the source, go to God." It sent a chill down his spine.

John opened his eyes, hoping the boys would be gone. Instead, they were closer than ever. One of them reached in and grabbed him by his collar and jerked him toward the window.

"You telling the truth? Tell me the number again."

Somewhere behind the boys, John heard a gun cock. The boys turned, and an old, short Hispanic man with bushy gray eyebrows had a rifle pointed at them. "¡*Suelte el arma!*"

The boy with the gun dropped it.

"And throw down the wallet. And the money."

The other boy dropped the wallet and credit cards.

"Now get your drug-dealing asses out of my neighborhood... And don't come back."

John saw the two boys run toward a parked car, jump in, and drive off. He looked back at the man with the gun. He was handing John his wallet and credit cards. "What you doing here, man?"

John took a deep breath and pointed to the house. "I...I grew up in that house."

"¿*Que*? You what?"

"I...I grew up there."

"That house?"

"Yeah. Until I was eight."

"No? 3337?""Yeah. Until I was eight."

"That is my house. Wait. Your dad a man named Tom Money? And mother, Ida?"

"That's them. How did you...

"And, I can't believe it. You're little John?"

"No one's called me that in...how did you know?"

"I bought this house from your dad. I paid $103 a month on the mortgage for thirty years."

John looked at him carefully. "You've lived here all that time?"

"And three kids." The old man looked toward the house. "It doesn't look as good any more. But my wife and I, we're over eighty now. I can't work in the yard anymore."

John opened the van door and stepped out. "Did I thank you? Can I shake your hand? What's your name?"

"Mario. Mario Garcia."

John reached out and shook Mario's hand. "Thanks."

"You're welcome. This isn't how we usually welcome visitors. Really, this is a quiet neighborhood, but those druggies come by, and we have to scare them off. You were in the wrong place at the wrong time."

John almost laughed. "I don't know. Someone told me that everything happens for a reason."

"Hard to believe you are little John. Want to come in and see the house? It looks better on the inside."

"No, thanks. I'll just remember it as it was."

"So, little John, why did you come here today?"

John shook his head. "I'm not sure. I guess I was searching for something."

"Searching? For what?"

"Answers, I suppose. I don't know."

The old man shrugged. "Answers? Here? I don't think there are many answers here anymore. I think you'll have to look someplace else."

"Yeah? Got any idea where?"

The old man's brow wrinkled in thought. "I only know one place that has answers."

"And that would be?"

Mario smiled. "Like my father used to tell me, whenever you need help, go to the source. Talk to God."

"Like my father used to tell me, whenever you need help,
go to the source. Talk to God."

Chapter 17

John left his old neighborhood and drove the rattletrap back to the freeway. He knew where he had to go. He took a familiar exit and saw the spire of his family's church sticking up in the distance like a lighthouse. After the VW bus pulled over to the curb in front of the church and stopped, John's head fell into the steering wheel. For a long few moments he didn't move. The street was silent. No cars passed by. No one walked along the sidewalk. *Maybe I'm dead already,* he thought. *Was that encounter with Lucky real? Maybe this was some kind of trick God was playing on him. Maybe this was hell already.*

John sat up, opened the bus door, and stepped out into the street. He looked up the concrete steps that led to the church sanctuary. Its tall columns loomed skyward. As a little kid, he'd slid down these banisters a hundred times. He'd played the part of Joseph in a live nativity one Christmas Eve in a manger at the top of the stairs. *He wasn't a heathen, after all. He'd gone to church all his life. Didn't those Sundays mean anything?*

As he stepped slowly up the stairs, his feet felt like lead. When he made it to one of the glass doors, he reached for the handle and pulled on it. The door was locked. No surprise. He stepped to the center door and pulled on it with the same result. He turned to walk back down the steps and didn't see someone come up on his right.

"Can I give you a hand there?"

John almost jumped out of his skin. He looked and saw an old man in coveralls holding a bucket and broom. John didn't recognize him and thought he must be the new church caretaker.

"Sorry, I didn't mean to startle you. Need some help?"

"No. No, everything is fine. Thanks." John turned to walk down the stairs.

"Really?"

John turned back to the old man. "Funny isn't it."

"Funny?"

"That we have all-night bowling alleys, but we lock up our churches."

The caretaker laughed.

John shook his head. "Says something about us, I guess."

The old man stepped to the center door and reached for the handle. "I suppose you tried this one."

"I tried that one, too, and it's..."

The door opened, and the caretaker smiled at John. "Seems open to me."

John looked suspiciously at him and then at the open door. "I know it was—"

"—must have just been stuck."

John walked up to the door and tentatively looked into the foyer. "Must have."

The caretaker opened the door a little wider. "You know, you're right. God's house should always be open. Never know when a fella might need to talk to the Lord about something. This has always been the place to get answers."

John didn't move.

"It's okay, go on in. He's home."

John stepped up to the door, paused, and then stepped inside the church. The caretaker closed the door behind him.

John squinted as his eyes grew accustomed to the bright sunlight filtering into the sanctuary through large stained-glass windows. He looked around. He was alone. He walked halfway down the aisle. It was the same room he'd visited almost weekly since childhood. But something was different. His knees almost gave way, and he grabbed the back of a pew to hold himself up. He felt his heart pounding, and he closed his eyes.

When he opened them again, his eyes were drawn to the stained-glass windows that lined the walls. On his right, he saw the window with the picture of the Good Shepherd tending sheep. He looked at the next window, Mary sitting at the feet of Jesus, with Martha staring at them from the background. The next window was the Good Samaritan helping a man who had been beaten. The last window on the wall to his right was a picture of Jesus knocking at a door. John never really understood that window. His eyes moved to the windows on the other side of the room. There, he saw Jesus kneeling in the Garden of Gethsemane. He thought about how Jesus also knew that his death would come soon. He'd asked the Father to take away the cup of death and allow him to live. But Jesus died.

John stepped forward to look more closely at the window. The sunlight streaming through the glass shouted at him in dazzling colors. *God didn't even answer His own Son's plea for life,* thought John. The image suddenly repulsed him. He looked away, clenched his fist, and shouted, "This is stupid."

The sound reverberated through the empty room.

He turned and shook his fist at the window. "What am I doing here? Did I come here for you? For me? For now? Forever? Why are you doing this to me?"

He stared at the window as if expecting an answer. None came. He shouted at the window again, "What do you want from me? Do you think I can do twelve good deeds in one day and make up for forty-seven bad years? What's supposed to happen? Do I say 'Hi, Jesus,' and you say 'Hi, John,' and then poof, we all live happily ever after?"

John exhaled. "No...I don't think so." He stood in silence.

A voice from behind him spoke. "Everything okay?"

John jumped, turned, and saw the caretaker standing inside the side door.

"Sorry. Guess my timing is a little off today. Didn't mean to spook ya. You all right? I thought I heard some shouting going on."

"Yeah...I'm okay. No...I'm not. I am definitely not okay."

"Anything I can do to help?"

"It's a little late for that."

"Late?" The caretaker looked at his watch. "It's only six thirty."

"No, I mean late for me. My time's up." John could see that his message didn't get through. "What I mean is that I lived my life, I took my chances, and now, here I am. My luck has run out. Now do you get it?"

The caretaker stepped toward John. "Son, I may not know much...but I do know that you are standing in the headquarters of one more chance."

"Forget it. Not for me."

"You wanna talk about it?"

"Do I know you?"

The caretaker extended his hand "You never know. Folks around here call me Guy."

By habit, John reached out and shook the caretaker's hand. "Well, hello, Guy, and you're the first I'll tell good-bye. You are looking at a dead man. A corpse in a suit. If I were you, I'd save your talk for someone who still believes in chances."

The caretaker shook his head. "I never waste a word on those with no hope."

"Then I bid you adieu." John turned to leave.

"You the one who gets to decide when there's no hope?"

John stopped and looked back. "Guy, I appreciate what you are trying to do, and I know where this is going."

"Really? Do tell."

"Save your breath, Guy. I've heard it." John pointed out to the empty room. "My family has been coming to this church for generations. See that pew over there? I sat there with my family every Sunday for as long as I can remember. And before me, my mom and dad sat there, and their parents before them. Are you getting this?"

The caretaker nodded.

John continued. "I've come through those doors and heard hundreds of sermons...and what good did it do?"

"Did you listen to any of them?"

"Please don't even...I mean, it's too late. I've spent this whole day trying to figure this out. Come on...I surrender, okay. Let's call it a day. I give up."

"Given up on who, you or God?"

"Both."

"Good thing you're not God. Because He'd never give up on you."

"Yeah, sure. I'll tell you what I know—that there's too little time left for me to do enough good deeds to make up for all the rotten things I've done in my life. No one can make up for a wasted lifetime in one night."

"Well, I've got to say that you're right about that."

John looked surprised at the answer. "Yeah, well...thank you."

"It's like the old saying 'Hell is full of people who thought they were doing good.'"

"That's exactly what I *didn't* want to hear."

"Listen, John, God's not interested in good deeds."

John smiled at the absurdity of it all. He sat down in the front pew. "So, you want me to believe that God is going to come down here, pat me on my head, perform some great miracle, and poof...all is forgiven, and everything is fine? Forget it."

"He already has."

"Excuse me?"

"The great miracle."

"What? What do you mean?"

"John, it's the miracle that frees you from all those years of bad decisions."

"Okay, you tell a good story, Guy, and if I had the time..."

"You do have time."

"Yeah, I wish."

He walked halfway down the aisle. It was the same room he'd visited
almost weekly since childhood

"Quit trying to earn heaven yourself. You're frustrated because it's impossible to do. You see that window over there?" The caretaker pointed to the Garden of Gethsemane window. "That's the night Jesus paid a big, big price to earn heaven for you." He turned and pointed to the opposite wall. "And see that one of Him knocking on the door? That's Him asking you to let Him in, so He can give you that free gift. John…"

John looked up. "Free gift?"

"Yes. Accept it; accept what God did for you…no strings, no catch. It's not about being good. It's about grace."

"That's what Morgan said earlier today."

"Morgan knows God."

"Yeah, she…"

"She knows that we're saved through our belief in God. There's nothing in this whole wide world you can do to earn it or deserve it. It's free."

"Listen, Guy, I've heard all this for years, but…"

"Maybe you have heard the words, but have you really listened…and believed them."

"You have no idea what I've done in my lifetime."

"I don't need to know what you've done. Everyone's done bad things in their lives, even evil things, things you don't want anyone to know about. But God knows about them, and he loves you anyway. And He still offers you a chance to join Him in heaven. That's why they call it grace. It's free for everyone…anyone."

John turned and looked at the Garden window, then back at Guy. "You really mean it? You really mean there's grace…for me?"

"Tonight, especially for you, John."

"I don't know. You make it sound so simple. I mean…"

"It is simple, John…simple as opening a door." The caretaker reached over a pew and pulled a Bible out of its pocket. He flipped through the pages until he found what he was looking for. "Do you remember ever hearing this verse, John? 'If you confess with your mouth that Jesus is Lord, and believe in your heart that God raised Him from the dead, you will be saved.'"

"It is simple, John...
simple as opening a door."

"Wait a minute. That's what Mandy said."

"That's because Mandy knows God, John. Now, it's your turn."

"You mean me? Confess? And believe? And that's it? How can it be that simple? There has to be more to it than that."

"Man makes it hard, John. See Jesus knocking at the door? He's asking for you to reach out and open the door. That's all you have to do. Open the door. Believe. Let Him in."

"Wait. Why am I just now hearing this? Why did it take forty-seven years and a death sentence?"

"Maybe it took something dramatic to make you listen. Maybe you're giving up on solving everything by yourself, and you're finally hearing Him knock at your door."

Guy handed the Bible to John and took a step back. "I think it's time for you and Him to have a heart-to-heart. This is something you have to do on your own."

John took the Bible and stared at it. "But I..."

"I know. You have questions. That's good, because He's got answers. Go ahead. Go to the source. Ask away. He's big enough to handle whatever you can dish out." The caretaker smiled and walked across the room and out the side door.

John didn't move for a long time. He held onto the Bible in his hand and stared at the cross at the front of the room. His eyes followed the jagged edges of the stained glass that had been put together into a mosaic to form the cross. His life was like that glass, he thought. Broken. Jagged edges. Something you might throw away. It was as if he heard a voice tell him, "John, I can take the broken pieces of your life and put them together into something beautiful. Don't trust in yourself to do it. Let me. Let me have your life."

John turned and looked at the stained glass window of Jesus knocking at the door. "It's as easy as opening a door."

He stood and walked toward the altar. Here is where he had taken communion many times. It had been a tradition to him, nothing more. But now. Now he knelt at the altar seeking a truer communion than he'd ever thought possible. As he knelt, it occurred to him that for the first time in his life, he really believed that he was about to speak to the living holy God. And he expected God to be listening.

"I'm stupid," he said aloud. "I'm stupid, ignorant, hardheaded, belligerent. I admit it, God. I admit it. I've wasted my life. I heard about You and never listened. I don't want to die. But if I have to, I want to live my last hours as I should have lived all of my years. Forgive me. I open my heart to You."

John collapsed with his face on the altar. In the stillness and silence of the moment, all he could think of was the song he'd learned as a child. "Jesus loves me, this I know. For the Bible tells me so.,,"

"Jesus loves me, this I know. For the Bible tells me so.,,"

Chapter 18

When John stood, he saw no lightning bolts, heard no applause, and felt no tingling in his body. He smiled and glanced at his watch and knew that he still had precious little time to wrap up the loose ends of his life. He turned back to the Gethsemane window. "Thank You, Lord, thank You."

Before he could make it to the back of the room, the caretaker stepped out of the door. "You still here? You okay?"

John reached out a hand to the old man. "Okay? No, I'm not okay. I'm...I'm fantastic, Guy. Thanks to you, I am fantastic."

The caretaker took John's hand and they shook. "Hey, no thanks to me. I'm just a messenger, son. I just reminded you of what you'd already heard."

"But why was I so hardheaded? Why did it take so long? But now, I've got to go. So little time...to explain all this to some very special people."

John heard a familiar voice, but not the caretaker's.

"Wait a minute!"

He turned and looked into the balcony.

Lucky stood at the rail, a clipboard in one hand and a donut in the other. "There you are! I tell you what, John Money, you are one tough cookie to figure out."

John glanced at his watch, then back at Lucky in disbelief.

"I've been to the country club, the office, your accountant, your lawyer's office..." Lucky took a bite out of the donut. "...and the donut shop looking for you. I never dreamed of looking here." He looked heavenward. "Thanks for the tip. I mean, go figure. John Money in church...on a Monday! Please, this is one for the books."

"Wait, wait...wait a minute. What are you doing here?"

"I said I'd be back."

"Yeah, you said 9:48 tomorrow morning." John glanced at his watch again. "Not 7:04 tonight."

"Yeah, I know. Listen. I have something..."

The caretaker walked down the aisle far enough to see who John was talking to. "Oh. It's you. Evening, Lucky."

"Hey, Guy, how is it going?"

"Never better."

John looked back and forth at the two in confusion. He looked up at Lucky. "Now you can just back up a minute, mister." He turned back to the caretaker. "Hey, hold up. He saw you." John suddenly sighed and turned back to Lucky, "Oh, man, you almost had me there. For a second, I thought you were here again for me, early. So, it's Guy's time, huh? Does he know?"

Lucky shook his head.

"Well, that's okay. Trust me; if anybody's ever been ready for you, it's him."

"John, it's not Guy's time. We don't get one."

John looked around and realized that the caretaker had gone. "Wait a minute, we had a deal. You said tomorrow...wait. What we?"

Lucky smiled, "We."

"What do you mean *we*?"

"Like me and he, we."

"You and he? You and he? Guy is an..."

"Angel, right. Guardian variety...very respected. Knows his stuff...top notch...as a matter of fact...your guardian angel."

"Wait…wait. Let me follow you. My guardian angel?

"Yeah, Guy's been with you since the day you were born."

John was flustered. "No. Wait. What? Forty-seven years? Why am I just now seeing him?"

"Oh, you've seen him before."

"No. Now you're wrong. I'd remember someone like that."

"That car wreck last year just outside of Fort Worth…remember that?"

"Yeah, so?"

"A fellow pulled you and Vanessa out of the car just before the fire started."

"You're saying it was Guy?"

"It was Guy."

"No, hang on, that was a much younger man. And Black…"

Lucky smiled and set his clipboard down. "We're not bound by the same rules as you are." As John looked at him, he vanished.

"Here I am."

John turned and saw Lucky at the front of the church. He disappeared again.

John turned to his right and saw the homeless man he'd given the hundred dollars to. "God bless you," he said, then dissolved into nothingness.

Further to his right he saw one of the kids selling the candy. "Thanks, mister," she said and vanished.

He turned around and saw the Bible translator behind him. "We need people, prayers, and money." He vanished.

John turned to the left and saw the bald man that had helped him on the freeway. "Ka-thunk?" he asked, and vanished.

Back toward the front, he saw the Hispanic man who lives in his old house. "Whenever you need help, talk to God." He vanished.

John looked up and saw Lucky standing in the balcony. He picked up his clipboard. "Kind of cool, huh, John?"

John caught his breath. "No…kind of creepy. Don't ever, ever, ever do that anymore."

"Oh, well..." Lucky pointed at the Bible in John's hand. "Besides, you've heard it before. It's all in the book. You never know when you're in the presence of angels."

"Wait...I get it. I do remember. Once we were clear of the accident, I looked for him to say thanks, and he was gone. And that was Guy? I never had a chance to thank him."

"I think you just told him. Besides, your thanks doesn't belong to Guy. It only belongs to the Top."

"But if that's the case, then this isn't fair. I finally made the connection to forever, and you're...you're early. You said a day. I took you at your word. I mean, when you say a day to me, it means twenty-four hours. I don't know who winds your clock, but mine says I still have a few ticks left."

Lucky disappeared from the balcony and appeared next to John. He stood tapping his foot with his arms crossed like he was waiting for John to stop.

John didn't stop. "Come on, I stood at the foot of the cross and found out I'm forgiven and guaranteed an eternity of joy. I get it...but I need just a little time to spend my last hours with my family." John looked heavenward. "Lord, please."

"You done?"

"No, you said a day. I planned for a day. I want my day! You said, 'I'll be back tomorrow.' You never said tonight. Tomorrow means tomorrow."

"Look, I know what I said..."

"What about Vanessa? What about Kelly and this Denver guy?"

"John...sometimes..."

"...and Mandy. What about Mandy? This is not right. I can't leave now. I have to let them know it's okay. I have to let them know I'll be waiting for them, and we will be together forever. You have to fix this..."

John reached into his pocket and produced his cell phone. "Here, call whoever called you this morning. You have to work this out. I mean..."

Lucky held up his hand. "Hold up. Listen to me. Stop. Cease. Desist! You have your time."

"And that's all I asked for...okay? Now if you'll step aside, I'll see you in the morning. Then I'll be ready to go."

John moved past Lucky toward the door.

Lucky followed John and tapped him on the back. "Mooney."

John turned and looked back, confused. "Excuse me?"

Lucky sighed. "Mooney. Mooney. Mooney. M-O-O-N-E-Y. It was Mooney! John A. Mooney, a ninety-seven-year-old guy three streets over from you. That was my pickup. Nice guy."

"Wait, you mean…"

"Yeah, it's not your time."

John smiled, then frowned, worried that he'd misunderstood. "Not my time?"

"Not your time."

"This is fantastic...but, how...why…when…?"

Lucky held out his clipboard, and John could see that it was smudged with grape donut filling.

"You know, records got smudged somehow. Mooney looked like Money...same zip code. I mean, hey, it can happen. I just call it an oops!"

"You call it an oops! I call it a miracle. Lucky, because of your "oops" I've found my way home."

Lucky shrugged. "Okay."

"I finally get it. Life's not about religion or doing good or going to church or any of those things. It's about a relationship with God...knowing and loving Him. That's why people do good deeds, because they love God! This is incredible! Wait till I tell Vanessa and the kids. And at the office,. Whoa are they in for a shock. I'm going to spend more time with my family. I'll make Ricky the new Marketing manager. And you know what, Lucky?"

"No, what?"

"For the first time in my life, I'm not afraid of dying. I mean death has no victory...it's just a doorway."

"Okay..."

"Hold on, there's more..."

"Oh, goody. I figured."

"It makes me want to live my life to the fullest! I'll be at every one of Mandy's dance recitals, and when Kelly goes off to learn her french fry language, I'll be there to send her off."

"French fries?"

"...and Vanessa, I'm taking her on a second honeymoon—to Maui. It's where she's always wanted to go. I'm gonna talk to the PTA. I'm gonna spend my time..."

"I get it. You are one happy fella."

"Happy? Are you nuts? This goes to another planet than happy. This is salvation. I'm free, I'm complete, and I'm delivered...set free!"

"And I am delighted, really."

He reached out and hugged Lucky. Lucky pushed John away and brushed himself off.

"And it is all because of you, Lucky."

"Yeah, yeah I got it. You're ecstatic. Listen, this is not how I usually interact with clients. I mean…"

"How can I ever thank you?"

"I can tell you this…we can start with no more of this love-in business. I have a reputation to uphold. After all, I am the Angel of Death."

John smiled. He moved toward Lucky for another hug. Lucky motioned him off.

"Okay, sure. You're welcome. I mean, anytime I can make a mistake, it is my pleasure to serve."

"Come on, we all know there are no mistakes with God."

Lucky nodded. "You know, you may be on to something. Even angels get surprised sometimes."

John extended his hand for a shake, and Lucky looked at him suspiciously. "Won't you even shake my hand?"

Lucky slowly raised his hand, and they shook. When they did, John pulled himself in and hugged Lucky again.

Lucky pulled away quickly, flabbergasted. He dropped to a karate position, pointing his fingers at John like he was going to zap him. "Did we not just talk about this? Don't make me..."

John backed off. And laughed. "Okay, hold your fire. I get it. But thanks...you saved my life."

Lucky dusted himself off, "Hmmm...Maybe I did." He looked toward heaven. "Well, I mean maybe I helped. Wow, first time for everything, huh? Well, listen, John, it was a great party, but I have some other pickups to deal with. So, you know, I guess I better fly. But hey, I will be seeing you later..."

"There's no hurry. Really, take your time. Oh, wait…" John smiled broadly and reached into his coat pocket.

Lucky turned back as John pulled out the bag of candy he'd bought from the two girls. "I almost forgot. You said you liked these."

John tossed Lucky the bag of truffles. Lucky caught them and smiled. "Mmmm...now we are talking heaven."

John blinked, and Lucky was gone. He looked again at the cross, turned and walked out the front door of the church. John heard Mandy's voice.

"Dad?"

Vanessa, Mandy, Kelly, and Austin were coming up the stairs. When they saw John, they all rushed up to him, and John welcomed them with a family hug.

After a moment, Vanessa stepped back and put her hands on her hips. "We've been looking all over for you! What in the world is going on?"

Mandy held on to her father's arm. "Yeah, Dad...we were worried about you."

Kelly stood next to Austin. "You scared us to death, Dad."

"Are you all right, sir?"

John smiled. "No, Austin, I am not."

They all looked confused.

"I am fantastic! You are not going to believe the day I've had. Let's go home, and I'll tell you all about it."

They turned and started down the stairs just as a black Mercedes approached the church. It stopped, and the window rolled down. Ricky stuck his head out and waved. Beth looked around him and also waved. Kaitlyn and Noah waved from the back window.

Vanessa watched the Mercedes pass by. She turned to John and put her hands on her hips. "John Money, what on earth has happened to our car?"

The Money Family at Home

NOTE TO THE READER:
For more information on stories and movies
by these authors, go to

http://www.alanelliott.com/novels

www.ingramcontent.com/pod-product-compliance
Lightning Source LLC
Chambersburg PA
CBHW060634130626
46555CB00002B/802